A Vineyard White Christmas

The Vineyard Sunset Series

Katie Winters

D0711741

Chapter One

It wasn't enough to be the black sheep of the family. Andrew Montgomery, the broad-shouldered and sinfully handsome son of Trevor Montgomery, was also the wildest. If life was a game of Texas Hold'em, he was all in. No question.

Eighteen years old and in the prime of everything, he flung his thumb out in the blisteringly chilly rain outside of Falmouth and waited for a car to pass. Beside him, his best friend on the planet, Kurt Leopold, yelped and called for the cars to stop.

"Come on, man! You got spare room!"

"If we don't get a ride soon, we're going to be late to the gig," Andy said under his breath. He lifted his thumb just the tiniest bit higher, arched it just-so, and suddenly, a little beat-up red car tore to the side of the road. The driver opened the window to reveal himself: a mid-forties guy with grizzled hair. He'd probably done a fair bit of hitchhiking back in his day.

"Where you boys off to?" he asked.

Before they knew it, Kurt and Andrew were stationed in the older guy's Toyota: Andrew in the passenger and Kurt in the back. They had never snuck off the island like this. They'd stolen Andrew's father's boat, hustled across the Sound, and parked up on one of the free docks, barren now that it wasn't the summer season.

"We're going to a gig in Boston," Kurt said.

"That right? Which gig?"

"Blink-182," Andrew said.

"Ah..." The older man adjusted in the driver's seat. His eyes were hazy with nostalgia. "*Nobody likes you when you're twenty-three.* That song?"

"Yep. They do that one and loads of others," Kurt said.

"They're one of our all-time favorite bands," Andy added.

"If only the other Kurt hadn't left this world," Kurt added. "Nirvana would have been my number one show."

"Now, that's what I'm talking about," the older man said with a smack across his heart. "Kurt Cobain was my life roundabout ten years ago. And it's just your luck, you know? I'm headed to Boston myself. But you boys better not hitchhike like this again. Not that you'd listen to an old guy like me. Where is it you live? Here in Falmouth?"

Kurt and Andy made heavy eye contact in the darkening air. Finally, Kurt said, "We live on the Vineyard."

"No way!" the man said. "I love the Vineyard. Of course, I haven't made it over there since I was a janitor for a while at one of the bed and breakfasts. Those summers over there were magical, some of the best times of my life. In the eighties, every single summer was the summer of love."

Andy and Kurt laughed appreciatively, grateful they hadn't stumbled into a serial killer's car.

"Do your parents know you're headed to Boston tonight?" the man asked, taking a quick look at Andrew. "I can't imagine you guys are anywhere past twenty. Ah, but it isn't my business, is it? When I was a teenager, all I wanted in the world was to get away from where I was from. The minute I was allowed,

I burst out the door without looking back. Tell you the truth, I kind of regret it. I don't think I knew what I had."

They sat in silence for the rest of the ride. Andrew and Kurt had planned this escapade over the last two months. In teenager-time, two months was a lifetime. They hadn't thought this night would ever come.

After their driver released them onto the frantic streets of Boston, they stood with their eyes wide and their hearts pumping with adrenaline. Twenty-somethings ambled around them in states of drunkenness, their arms flung around one another. It was the end of January, and the air hovered right between freezing and not: hence the rain.

Andrew produced their tickets at the door, where they showed the fake IDs they had purchased from a kid at school who knew a guy. The door guy hardly grunted at the IDs before he tilted his head toward the door. By the time five minutes passed, Andrew and Kurt had cheap beers in their hands. They were headed toward the front of the crowd.

Andrew had never seen a world like this one. In fact, he had hardly been off the Vineyard his entire life. His father, Trevor Montgomery, and his mother, Kerry Montgomery, were the top-billed real estate brokers on Martha's Vineyard, which meant they wanted nothing that the Vineyard couldn't give them. Frequently, Andrew stumbled into his father finalizing property deals with celebrities in their fancy dining room, the one they never used. A few weeks ago, Brad Pitt and Jennifer Aniston had laughed with Trevor Montgomery over three cans of Fresca like they'd known one another for years.

The concert hall was filled with classic punks. Green mohawks, nose rings, bad tattoos, the kinds of people Andrew's father would have said were "trashy or losers," and the kinds of things Andrew probably would have gone for if he didn't think his mother would have had a stroke.

"Look at how hot that girl is," Kurt muttered into Andrew's ear.

Andrew said, "Yeah, wow," even though he didn't know which girl Kurt referred to. Every girl in there looked the same to him.

The concert began with an opener that nobody paid attention to except Andrew and Kurt. They had traveled all that way for the first real gig of their lives and wanted to focus on every single second of it, even if it hurt their eyes to do it. When Blink strummed their guitars for the first time, Andrew's heart shattered into a million pieces. Whatever emotion these guys gave him, he wanted to follow that emotion for his entire life.

It had nothing to do with the stuffy life on Martha's Vineyard that he had begun to hate. It had nothing to do with the boxed-in life his father wanted him to live.

* * *

Just after one in the morning, Andrew and Kurt scrambled back on Andrew's father's boat and revved the engine. Andrew zipped his coat all the way to his chin as he clutched the steering wheel with a gloved hand. The air that rippled over the Sound felt like needles.

"That show changed my life, man," Kurt howled over the sound of the motor. "I'll never forget it as long as I live."

"Me neither!" Andrew called.

When they reached the center darkness of the Sound, Andrew stopped the engine. He hadn't expected himself to do it. There was just something about the way you couldn't see where the night sky changed to the water beneath them, as though they existed inside a black globe, with the stars twinkling above.

"Do you think you'll leave the Vineyard?" Andrew asked Kurt then.

Kurt collapsed to the side of the boat, grabbed a beer they had stocked, and cracked it open. "What do you mean? Like, after graduation?"

"Yeah, I guess."

"Man, I don't know," he replied. "Nobody in my family ever has. And you heard that guy who drove us up to Boston. People crave the life we have."

The waves pulsed against the boat and tilted it to-and-fro.

"My dad is so intense sometimes," Andrew said. "I worry that if I don't leave, I'll never get out from under him, you know?"

"He can be a real SOB sometimes," Kurt agreed.

Andrew chuckled. "But then again, I think about my siblings. Steven already has Jonathon and Isabella. Kelli has three kids, with Lexi just a baby. I know Charlotte and Claire are itching to have babies with Jason and Russell. I don't want to miss them growing up."

"You want to be Uncle Andy?" Kurt asked. A grin splayed across his face.

"Sure. Who wouldn't want that?"

"I guess you're right. If Beth has kids, I want to be around for that."

Andrew's eyes flashed at the sound of Beth Leopold's name. She was a raven-haired beauty, no more than five-foot-one, with glowing green eyes and an easy, expressive laugh. At just one year younger than Kurt, she had chased at their coat-tails for as long as either of them could remember. Andrew couldn't pinpoint exactly when he had fallen for her, though; it had unfurled from his heart one summery day, maybe, when he'd realized he wanted no life without her.

The thing of it was, now that she was seventeen, she had a boyfriend.

Andrew shoved his hands deep into his pockets, hidden from the chilly wind. Before long, they latched themselves to the side of the Montgomery family dock. Both Andrew and Kurt had flung themselves off of this very dock time and time again, summer after summer, as they laughed up to the blissful blue sky above.

"Thanks for one of the wildest nights of my life," Kurt whispered as he walked away from the dock and back toward his house, only a few streets away. "I'll never forget it—ever."

Andrew hustled to the screened-in porch that overlooked the dock and the Vineyard Sound. Tentatively, he cracked open the screen door as gently as possible, grateful that the house was dark and shadowed. Nobody noticed he hadn't come home before curfew.

Or at least, that's what they wanted him to think.

When he opened the porch door that led into the kitchen, he found his father at the kitchen table with a book in his hands and a small candle flickering beside him. For a long time, Andrew hovered in the doorway, his mouth gaping open. It was almost like his father was a ghost.

Finally, Trevor Montgomery closed his book slowly, turned his eyes toward his youngest son, and said, in an ominous voice, "Andrew, won't you close the door? It's January, and you're freezing up the house."

It didn't take long for the ax to fall.

"What on earth were you thinking? Your mother is half-sick with worry, but I told her, our Andrew? Our Andrew is just being a fool, but he's also smart as a whip when he chooses. He knew just what to do to get himself out of here and just what to do to slip right back. The thing of it is, Andrew, I'm pretty smart, too. I caught wind of your little trip. I hope you're happy. I hope you had a damn good time. Because son? If you ever do anything like this again, you'll be out of this house in a damn flash. Do you hear me?"

A wave of darkness fell over Andrew's face. He found it difficult to answer.

What did he want to say, exactly? Something like: *If you made it easier to talk to you, maybe I would have asked if I could go. Oh, no, wait. That wouldn't have worked, either, because you refuse to listen to anything I ask or say. You don't care. You already had four children and me? I was the mistake, wasn't I? God forbid you have any time left for me. You want me out of the house just as much as I want to go.*

Just as he opened his lips, his mother appeared in the kitchen doorway. She adjusted the belt of her fuzzy pink robe and blinked sleepily.

"Why doesn't everybody head to bed?" she whispered. "It's almost three in the morning. Nothing good happens at this time of the night."

Chapter Two

Trevor Montgomery didn't look at his son Andrew for a good two months after that— he was always known for being a little too bitter. But Andrew knew that having a son involved in sports was currency, especially on Martha's Vineyard, and Trevor began to greet Andrew with high-fives and pats-on-the-back as the season's first game grew closer to spring.

"There he is. My star pitcher!" he called, sometimes even from his fancy car as he drove past with celebrities in the passenger side, ready to look at properties.

Andrew loved baseball. Throughout his younger years, his older and only brother, Steven, had taught him almost everything he knew now. He had stood out in the yard near the Vineyard Sound and played catch with him, adjusted his stance, and helped him to focus. Steven was now thirty years old; his eldest son was now seven. This left Andrew to teach Jonathon everything Steven himself had taught him about baseball, especially since Steven was busy at the auto shop. *"When it comes time for you to provide for a family, Andy, you'll be just as exhausted as I am now. I can't find the energy to do anything but eat and sleep,"* Steven had told him recently.

The first five or so games of the season went better than okay. The local newspaper interviewed Andrew several times about his performance and called him "Martha's Vineyard's Greatest Athlete." Everything seemed to simmer with potential, especially after a college scout called him and said, "I can't believe we missed out on you last year. We might be interested in having you come play with us next school year."

All that changed when Andrew and Kurt were caught drinking out behind the baseball diamonds on a beautiful April night. Andrew was halfway through a fifth of whiskey, and Kurt had fought his way through about seven beers so far. Apparently, their screamed lyrics of the Goo Goo Dolls song they loved so much had alerted the neighbors, and the police had responded.

"Dad's so mad," Andrew said at Steven's dinner table.

Steven cast him a dark look and gestured toward Jonathon, who played on the floor with a selection of plastic dinosaurs.

"Sorry. I mean, Dad's never going to forgive me for this. Better?" Andrew asked.

"I guess. And you know that's not true," Steven said. He opened the refrigerator, grabbed two beers, and placed one in front of Andrew. As he sat across from him at his kitchen table, the smell of the auto shop wafted in the air around him.

"You sure you want to give me one of these?" Andrew asked, arching an eyebrow.

Steven shrugged. "You've had a long day. Dad probably tore your ear off. I think you deserve it."

Andrew popped the top off his beer just as Jonathon hustled up with a dinosaur toy.

"Uncle Andy! Do you know what this dinosaur is called?" he asked.

"I don't, Jon. Tell me," Andrew said.

"It's called a Brachiosaurus," Jonathon said. "Do you want to know what that means?"

"I think you're gonna tell me," Andrew said with a laugh.

"It means 'arm lizard,'" Jonathon explained. "They lived during the mid- to late Jurassic Period, and they've mostly been found in North America, which is where we are."

"Almost right, Jon," Andrew said. "We're actually on an itsy-bitsy island alongside North America. I imagine there weren't that many Brachiosaurus here."

Jonathon's smile crumpled, which resulted in instant proof of Andrew's mistake.

"Shoot, I mean. Well, I'm sure there were at least a few of them," Andrew corrected himself. "I'm sure some of the Brachiosaurus saw our little Vineyard and thought, hey! Maybe we could camp up there. Build our fancy houses and eat our caviar and..."

Jonathon tumbled back on the floor and busied himself with his dinosaurs again. Andrew shrugged at Steven and added, "I guess he doesn't care about my scientific analysis of Martha's Vineyard."

"Most people don't, Andy," Steven said. "Where did that hatred come from, anyway? I never remember you having it out for the Vineyard when you were younger."

Andrew considered this. He tilted the beer bottle in his hand and remembered the blissful summers, the wild nights, and the cozy winters on his mother's lap while she read him a bedtime story.

"I don't." The words tumbled out of his lips before he could stop them. "I don't."

Steven furrowed his brow. "Then what's the problem?"

Andrew took a long sip of beer. "Mom and Dad just really want to be done with me. They don't see me the way they see you, Kelli, Charlotte, and Claire. I was a tag-on. A mistake. And now, I've messed up yet again."

"Come on. Almost all of us got in trouble for drinking as kids," Steven said.

"Well, I don't think Mom and Dad remember that," Andrew said. "And with my luck, they'll only remember my mistakes. Their final problem child. The black sheep. The one who made them look bad and tarnished their perfect reputation."

"None of us could have known their real estate company would have taken off the way it did," Steven affirmed. "Their quality of life has shifted in the past years."

Andrew shrugged. "So you admit it. They're different. And they need me gone."

That minute, Steven's wife, Laura, appeared in the kitchen. She rubbed Steven's shoulder softly and gave Andrew a guarded, yet still friendly, smile. She looked like she wanted to say something about the beer but didn't.

"Hey Andy," she said. "How's the end of senior year going?"

"It's going, I guess. One accident at a time," Andrew said, then took a long swig from his beer.

"Well, you'll get to the end, I guess. And then you'll look back and say these were the best years of your life," Laura said. "You're so free. You don't have to pay bills or nag little boys to brush their teeth."

Jonathon froze on the carpet. Slowly, he tilted his head to face his mother, who arched her eyebrows playfully. "That's right, Jonathon Montgomery. It's time for you to get ready for bed."

"I don't think so," Jonathon affirmed. "I still have about two hours left of my game."

"Aren't you the inventor of your game? It seems to me you can stop it now and start it back up again tomorrow," Laura said.

Jonathon stuck out his lower lip ominously. Over the years,

Andrew had heard the kid perform some gut-wrenching screams, the kinds of things that deserved Oscars. This time, however, Steven bolted toward his son, grabbed him beneath his armpits, and tossed him in the air. The boy's bad humor immediately switched as he yelped, giggled, and romped.

"Steve! You're going to get him all wound up," Laura said, standing with her hands on her hips. She gave her husband a warning glare.

But Steven didn't care, and Jonathon looked like he floated on air. When he fell again into his father's arms, he placed a kiss on his scruffy cheek and said, "You smell like cars, Daddy."

Like a spell, he was ready to go to bed.

"I always smell like cars," Steven said as he winked toward Andrew. "Your mother loves it."

Steven whisked Jonathon up the steps. There was the sound of his footsteps as he stepped toward the bathroom; there was the sound of the sink as Steven instructed Jonathon on how to brush his teeth. Laura cleared her throat over the top of the table and gave Andrew a look that meant, *Shouldn't you be headed back home?*

Andrew took another swig of his beer and stood. "Thanks again for your hospitality, Laura. I'll see you soon."

"Keep your chin up, kid," Laura said. "We're all rooting for you."

Her words followed Andrew back out into the April night. Graduation was a little over six weeks away, and it felt like the strangest finish line, one with a large hazy "what if" after it. Andrew zipped up his spring jacket and headed down the sidewalk with his hands crammed in his pockets. In just another week, he would be allowed back on the baseball field; in just another week, his pitches would whip through the air again.

But that college scholarship? It wasn't on offer anymore.

Instead of heading straight home, Andrew paused outside his sister Kelli's house. There, she lived with her husband,

Mike, their son, Sam, aged four, their other son, Josh, aged two, and their daughter, Lexi, who had been born in early January. Mike also worked in real estate—sometimes under their parents. Kelli was now twenty-eight years old, a responsible mother, and a business owner in her own right. She had opened a little boutique down the road the previous summer, which had become a success.

Andrew loved all his siblings, but for reasons he had never understood, he loved Kelli the most. He supposed it was because she'd always been the kindest and always let him pour his heart out without being judgmental. She'd sat up with him long nights some fifteen years ago: reading him stories and swapping out the names for his name and her name. When she'd been a teenager, in the midst of dating, he hadn't liked any of her boyfriends. He had been surprised to find that he hated the man she had chosen for her husband even more.

How had such a beautiful, intelligent, kind creature found any kind of love in Mike Williams?

Andrew knew that Kelli's door was always open for him. He headed up the walkway that led to their front door, lifted his hand, and prepared to rap his knuckles.

At that moment, Mike's voice rattled through the house.

"What the hell were you thinking, Kelli? Are you serious right now?"

Andrew froze. There was a loud, horrible sound, like the sound of someone throwing something across the room.

"Mike, please. You'll wake the baby."

"*Mike, please. You'll wake the baby,*" Mike imitated her. "Do you hear yourself? You sound pathetic. Just admit it. You were flirting with him today when I came in. Weren't you?"

"No! I swear. I was just catching up. I haven't seen him since high school, and..."

"I saw it in your eyes. You wanted him, Kelli. Admit it."

"I love you, Mike. You're jealous, and you're selfish, but I..."

"Shut up!"

Andrew froze with rage. That moment, the baby wailed from wherever she lay, somewhere in the front room. The light snapped on, and Andrew ducked down just as Kelli stepped into the room to collect Lexi and soothe her. He tried the door; he wanted to check on her, but it was locked.

"Shh, honey. It's okay," Kelli breathed.

"Whatever," Mike called from the back room. "I'm going to bed."

Andrew listened as his horrible brother-in-law stomped up the staircase, leaving his wife and their howling daughter below. When Andrew was sure Mike had gone, he rapped delicately at the door until Kelli cracked it open to find him standing in front of her. Kelli's eyes were hollow, as though she couldn't see him at all.

"Andrew, what are you doing here?" she rasped.

"I wanted to say hello." Andrew righted himself and tried to give her a smile, but it failed. "Are you okay?"

"What? Of course I'm okay," she returned.

"I just...I heard something and, well," Andrew trailed off.

In Kelli's arms, Lexi turned over to burrow her head between her arm and chest. It was painfully cute. Andrew's heart surged with love for the little thing.

"Do you want anything? Some cereal?" Kelli asked. "I'm sorry I haven't reached out after the whole baseball thing. It sounds so hard, though. You and Kurt always seem to get into so much trouble."

Andrew gave a sad shrug. He didn't want to leave her. Not while she looked so sad. "Sure. I'll take some cereal."

He found himself at her little kitchen table while she placed her daughter tenderly back in the bassinet. With tired arms, she poured them both bowls of Lucky Charms cereal, with just the tiniest bit of milk, just the way they'd always liked it.

"Mike doesn't like it when I buy the name-brand cereal," she said as she sat across from him. "So I hide it in the back of the cupboard. He never looks, and Sam loves it the best."

"Me too," Andrew said. His spoon hovered over the glorious fake marshmallows and the little crunchy delights. He looked at his sister, really looked at her: at the hollow circles that sat beneath her eyes and the start of frown lines that crept up between her eyebrows. "You'd tell me if you need help, right?" he asked.

Kelli pondered this as she chewed her first bite of cereal. "I just don't know what you could do, Andy."

This stung. Andrew blinked back tears that had now formed. "I'm not a kid anymore," he told her. "I'm about to graduate. And you don't have to do this. Whatever it is."

Kelli heaved a sigh. "In many ways, I still feel like a kid, maybe even younger than you. But it's all much more complicated than I could have anticipated. Fights mean a lot less than they used to. They just happen."

They just happen.

He didn't want to push the subject any further. He knew Kellie understood that he was there for her, that he knew her marriage was rocky at best with Michael. When he took one final glance at his sister, she looked exhausted, and so he made his way to the door. It was time to leave.

Andrew headed back to his house. His tongue was caked with the taste of sugary-sweet cereal. After he placed the key through the front door, he found only his mother in front of the television, with the remote control lifted.

"Oh, good. You're home," she said. "Dad was worried we would get yet another call that you were in trouble."

Chapter Three

"Congratulations to the class of 2003."

Principal Miller's voice roared through the loudspeaker as the students assembled across the football field and whipped their graduate hats toward a glorious blue sky. Andrew kept his in his hands and watched as the other graduate hats fluttered down around him, in odd directions, never landing back in the right place. With every thud of his heart, he knew: this was the end of something he would never get back. He wasn't sure what to do with that.

Kurt Leopold was just a few seats away from Andrew Montgomery. When they got the all-clear to head out on their "life adventures" alone, Kurt jumped toward Andrew and hugged him wildly.

"Man, we did it! We made it. I thought we would never do it, but here we are."

Andrew and Kurt walked together toward the bleachers, where their families waited for them in their Sunday best. Andrew caught his father's eyes as he approached; the man tried out a smile, but it looked odd on his face, especially since he hadn't managed a smile for his youngest son since the whole "drinking on the baseball field" incident.

Andrew's mother threw herself around Andrew and said, "Congratulations, honey. You looked great up there. We're so proud of you."

"You mean for the split-second that I marched across the stage?" Andrew asked.

"Come on, Little Bro," Steven said. He wrapped his arm around Andrew's shoulder and tugged him into a hug. "Don't give Mom a hard time."

"Thanks. Um." He swallowed the lump in his throat and added, "Thank you all for being here. It means a lot to me."

"Only an hour till the party starts," his mother said. "We'd better get back to finish setting everything up. All the Sheridans will be there, along with your father's family and all your friends."

Andrew's heart thudded with dread. He hated the concept of a graduation party: all those people smacking his shoulder, congratulating him, and telling him it was time for him to "become a great man like his father." Plus, there was all that pressure of it being a party. A time his parents had set aside to spend money on him, bring in nice cakes and fancy foods and coolers of beer for the family.

He had to clench his teeth and get through it.

After the party, the rest of his life would begin.

He wasn't so keen on that, either.

* * *

The party was elaborate, only the kind of thing the Montgomery family would put together to show off just how wealthy they had become in recent years. At least, that's how it seemed to Andrew. Everyone else was off to the races, having a good time. As his mother brought out the cake, Claire and

Charlotte rushed up to hug him again and rustle his hair, just as they had done when he was much younger.

"I can't believe it! You graduated!" Charlotte said as she leaned back into the arms of Jason, the love of her life.

"Fantastic work, man," Jason said. Like Steven with the auto shop, Jason always seemed to smell the tiniest bit like fish.

"Seriously, I hope you know we're proud of you," Claire said as she lowered her voice. "I know Dad has put a lot of pressure on you over the past year. But you have to know, it's just because there's been so much pressure on him and his career. All those big clients, looking to him for help. He still loves you, you know?"

Kurt and his sister, Beth, appeared on the far side of the party. Andrew's whole body sizzled with electricity at the sight of them.

"I'll catch you guys later," he told his sisters before he headed over, grabbing a few beers along the way. Who could stop him? It was his graduation, after all.

"Hey, man!" Kurt said. "Beth wanted to come. Hope that's cool."

"Of course," Andrew said. He smiled sheepishly at this beautiful, radiant girl, *the girl with the boyfriend,* and added, "Thanks for coming. Want a beer?"

"Thanks." Beth took it slowly and cracked it open. Her eyes told him something—something that intrigued him.

She liked him.

He knew it in his core.

"Lots of people are here," Kurt said as he scanned the crowd.

"My father made sure of that," Andrew said.

All the while, his eyes remained on Beth's.

"It's so weird to see your brother and sisters so much older now, with their own kids," Kurt continued.

"Tell me about it," Andrew said. To Beth, he said, "I'm Uncle Andy these days..."

"You must be the best uncle," Beth said. Her cheeks brightened to a pink shade. "I mean, they must love you a lot."

Andrew wasn't sure, in retrospect, how it happened. Inch by inch, second by second, somehow, he and Beth ended up alone in the corner of the backyard, both sipping beers, talking to each other in a way that made it feel as though they were the only two in the entire universe. Andrew had no idea where Kurt was; in fact, if asked at that moment, he might have said, "Kurt? Never heard of him."

Ultimately, he and Beth ended up together in the long hallway that led toward his bedroom: their lips pressed together, their breath hot and urgent.

Only then did his mother make a move for the stairwell to call up and say, "Andrew! All your guests are waiting down here. You have to say hello to everyone and thank them for stopping by."

Their kiss broke as Beth chuckled softly and stroked his face. "They always know, don't they?"

"That woman always has a pretty good hunch," Andrew whispered. "Can I find you after the party?"

"Of course."

Andrew cradled her tenderly for a long moment. Perplexed, he said, "I thought you had a boyfriend?"

Beth shrugged. "Things change, don't they?"

"I guess that's one of the only constants in this life," Andrew returned before walking back downstairs.

Andrew fell in line with his father, Steven, his Uncle Wes, and Jason. Jason spoke about a recent catch he had made out on the water, "the biggest trout he'd ever seen in his life." His father suggested that Andrew do a little internship with the fishing company that summer. "Something to get your hands dirty while you think about what you want to do next."

Andrew's stomach twisted up with nerves. He made eye contact with Jason as he said, "I'll have to think about that."

"It's no trouble if you're not interested," Jason said hurriedly. "I only mentioned it to your father because he said you struggled with what to do next. I said I don't think I would have known what to do if my parents hadn't owned this fishing company. I fell into it and it fit me like a glove. It doesn't fit everyone, of course."

Andrew wanted to give his father a dark look, one that translated just how little he liked his future discussed with random others. Instead, his Uncle Wes rapped him on the back and yanked his attention in that direction.

"But I also just told your father here that we always need extra staff at the Sunrise Cove over the summer," he said. "That place is difficult to keep up with, especially now that all the girls have run off to find themselves." His eyes grew hazy with sadness, even as his smile remained plastered on.

Andrew knew how much pain his Uncle Wes had gone through: from his wife's drowning to the one-by-one abandonment of Susan, then Christine, and then finally, Lola. Andrew's memories of the girls had grown blurry over the years. Susan had been nearly ten years older than him; she had left when he was only nine years old. It was said that she already had a family of her own in New Jersey.

"Thanks, but I'll have to think about that too, Uncle Wes," Andrew heard himself say.

His father's eyes grew stormy. "Andrew hasn't worked much the past year."

"I held down that lifeguard job till the end of the season," Andrew interjected.

"All you did was flirt with the tourist girls," his father insisted. "And get a good suntan."

Actually, I saved an older man's life. I tugged his lifeless form out of a particularly frantic wave and found him soggy and pale and almost lifeless. Only when I stretched him out on the beach did the water burst from his lips like a fountain.

"Right. Yep. That's all I did." Andrew felt on the verge of exploding. He gripped a beer from the cooler and twisted off the top a little too aggressively.

"Time for you to join the real world," his father said. "It's time for all these fun and games to come to an end."

Andrew had to escape his father's presence and found himself toward the side of the party as the moon strung itself up in the cavernous night sky. Conversations purred around one another and became a kind of beehive of sound. He couldn't articulate anything and had no desire to join a single conversation. Both Kurt and Beth had run off to another graduation party, both insisting that he catch up with them after his own guests left.

Andrew walked back into the side entrance of the large house to use the bathroom. In the darkness of the hallway, he heard hissing, bad language, and the kind of volatility that made the walls shake. He froze and focused on the words.

"You have no idea how you embarrassed me out there. Are you serious right now? I came all the way here to celebrate your loser brother's graduation, and this is how you treat me?"

Mike.

Andrew crept closer to the source. Mike and Kelli stood in the dark gray haze of the kitchen. Kelli had her hands stretched over her cheeks as Mike belittled her.

"You're pathetic," Mike blared. "I don't know what kind of example you think you're giving our children."

Andrew shoved himself the rest of the way into the kitchen with his fists raised. Before Mike had a chance to speak, he used all the anger that had generated over the previous hours to smash Mike directly in the nose. Mike fell back with a funny, childlike look smeared across his face. He landed against the counter and howled. Blood rained out of his nose.

"Andrew!" Kelli cried. She leaped for Mike—the man who had only just berated her!—and grabbed his shoulder to ask him if he was okay. Mike's eyes looked like malevolent gems.

Suddenly, Andrew's father burst in through the back door. His eyes went to Andrew, to Kelli, and then to Mike's bloody nose. In a split second, he knew exactly what had gone wrong.

"Andrew, what have you done?" his father demanded.

Andrew had no room for an apology. His hatred for Mike spread through his veins like a virus.

"Andrew. Come to my office. Now," his father growled. He stepped toward him, grabbed him by the upper arm, and dragged him toward the hallway like a little kid. All the while, Andrew turned his head back toward Mike. He wanted to give him a look that would tell Mike not to mess with his sister again; that punch wouldn't be his last.

Once inside Trevor Montgomery's office, Trevor grabbed a bottle of expensive whiskey with a shaking hand and poured himself two fingers. For a long time, he studied his glass and shook his head. Andrew heaved toward the side of the room as his adrenaline depleted.

"I hate him, Dad. You didn't hear what he said to Kelli. He..."

"I've thought it for a long time, son." Trevor's eyes lifted slowly.

"So you've heard what he's said to her?"

His father shook his head delicately. "No. Whatever's up with Kelli and Mike is between Kelli and Mike. But you? My youngest? The runt of the litter? I've thought about it for a long, long time, and I realized..." He took a long, horrible sip of whiskey. "You've really disgraced our family, son. I really don't know what to do with you."

The words felt like shrapnel. Andrew dropped his chin to his chest and blinked down at his ridiculous Italian-made shoes, the ones his mother had forced him to wear for graduation.

They pinched his toes horribly; a tension headache had started to form at the base of his skull.

"Wow. Well, at least now I know how you really feel. I guess there's nothing left to say," Andrew whispered as his eyes locked one final time with his fathers. He cast his eyes to the floor and stepped toward the door, slipped out into the hallway, and headed up toward his bedroom. Someday, much sooner than he'd ever anticipated, this wouldn't be his bedroom any longer.

Maybe it was better that way, after all.

Chapter Four

The first Boston apartment was rundown and bug-infested. Kurt and Andrew sat out on the leather couch they had bought from Craigslist and counted the cockroaches through the late evening and into the morning as they drank beer and spoke about what they would do next. The idea of the military revealed itself after a recruiter had approached them at the grocery store. "I guess we have that puppy dog look," is what Andrew said about it as he lifted the brochure. "We obviously don't know what to do next."

Money was tight; neither of them received enough hours at their jobs as a sandwich-maker and pool technician at the local YMCA. Before the end of August, they had signed up for the military, and by the middle of September, they had fallen fully in love with the idea of it all.

"Man, it's perfect. While we serve, we can think about what we really want our lives to be," Kurt said. "Then, they'll pay for our college. We can go together. Be roommates, even. We'll be, what? Twenty-four, twenty-five? By then, we'll know so much more, and we'll have served our country in the meantime. It's a win-win!"

It sounded right to Andrew. It was ideal to have something to look forward to, a goal he could prop up in front of his remaining sadness about his family and the life they'd left behind. Before they'd decided against paying for the phone bill, his mother had called every few days. Now, the silence that came off of Martha's Vineyard felt louder than ever. Every day, Andrew felt the ache in his heart grow. But none of that mattered now. He was a grown man, off to do what he wanted, and he was just as stubborn as his old man.

"Weird that we missed a whole summer there," Kurt said late one night as they packed up for their first training. "I always took them for granted."

"Sure, but it wasn't so bad up here," Andrew said. As the words tumbled out of his lips, he felt the density of the lie.

"I talked to Beth a few days ago," Kurt said.

Andrew's ears perked up. He hadn't seen Beth since she had driven them both up to Boston. Her eyes had been hollow when she'd said goodbye. *I thought we had something,* they'd seemed to say.

"How's she doing?"

"Good, I guess. Ready for senior year. She also asked if we're really sure about joining the army."

"I guess it's too late to back out now," Andrew said.

Kurt considered this. "You're right, and besides, it'll be an adventure, right?"

* * *

Months later, when Kurt and Andrew were stationed in Afghanistan, Andrew got up the courage to write his mother a letter. He was gut-wrenchingly homesick. So many men had died around him, and the air held a scent of death. It didn't

25

matter which way you turned; it was there, just lingering every-where. He missed the soft sea breezes; he missed his mother's clam chowder, her soft voice and gentle touch; he missed the tender beauty of the New England rain and his nieces and nephews running around, yelling at one another. Home was meant to be where the heart was, he thought. In his case, that wasn't always the truth. Either way, he was still homesick.

It was now 2004, which meant that any wild energy and anger for the devastation that happened on September 11, 2001 had whittled itself down and become strangely passive. War was what they did; war was all they had. As Andrew awaited a message back from his mother, he and Kurt snuck time together to talk about Martha's Vineyard and exchange old stories of what they had left behind.

"That night, when we were on the boat headed back from the Blink-182 concert," Kurt breathed. "I think about that night all the time. I thought the world was full of possibilities. As many possibilities as there were stars in the sky."

"Now we just have this," Andrew affirmed.

Kurt's eyes had become sunken with dark circles. They were stressed, going on zero sleep at times, with only their adrenaline to see them through. Andrew avoided mirrors, as he hated to imagine what had happened to his own appearance due to the stressors of war. They tried to keep one another's spirits light; naturally, it was difficult.

By the time Kerry Montgomery's letter reached Afghanistan, Kurt Leopold had been killed in the line of fire.

The attack had come out of nowhere. Andrew hadn't been on duty at the time; to think of it later, he'd been fast-asleep, dreaming of Martha's Vineyard summers and long days on the lifeguard stand, steaming beneath the sun. When someone jostled him awake to tell him the awful news, his grogginess made the impact of the story not as harsh or even a reality. It was only afterward, as he settled into the realization that his best friend from his childhood was now dead, that he began to weep uncontrollably.

Kurt's body had been shipped back to Martha's Vineyard shortly after. Only then did Andrew read his mother's letter. It was a list of the items she had grown in the garden that year, the things she'd done with her grandchildren, the excitement she had over Claire's engagement, that kind of thing. She didn't mention anything about when Andrew would return home; she also didn't bring up anything about what had happened between Andrew and his father. Hardened by battle and Kurt's death, Andrew resolved to take another tour. Martha's Vineyard had nothing for him, anyway.

Years passed. Andrew turned twenty-one, and then he turned twenty-three. He found himself moving up in rank, stationed in Iraq, Iran, back in Afghanistan, sometimes in Germany or France or wherever the army needed him. Through his travels, he saw much more of the world than he had ever envisioned from the safety of his Martha's Vineyard home. He took photos, but he had nobody to send them to. As social media became more in vogue, he contemplated making an account and reaching out to one of his sisters or his brother. That said, so much time had passed at this point; they had all lived without one another for so long that it seemed unnecessary that they put the time in to build any kind of relationship.

Once in a blue moon, Andrew returned to Boston for some rest and recuperation. Other soldiers hugged their wives and their children and their dogs; they went back to their cozy houses and their beautiful backyards and their enviable worries. Andrew had the same schedule every time he got back. He got a month-by-month rental apartment; he got out some of his things from storage; and he set up shop for a few months, watching sports on TV and hanging at the local bar. Nothing about his life was anything like he had pictured, but heck, he was a soldier through and through. He served his country.

Nobody could knock what he had done for his country. In fact, more often than not, people came up to him to thank him for his service.

From time to time, Andrew wondered what his father thought of his youngest "runt" son's decision to join the army. He could almost hear Trevor Montgomery say something like, *"That'll kick him into shape if nothing else does."*

Maybe this was it, Andrew thought to himself as he prepared for yet another tour in the Middle East. Maybe this was all life would ever be for him. Maybe it could be enough.

Chapter Five

Present Day – March

"That's right, Andrew. Just four more steps for me, and then you can take a break. Just four more."

Andrew winced as pain shot up and down his right leg. Just short of that final step, he gripped the railings on either side, gasped, and puffed out his cheeks. His tousled blond hair swept down around his ears as he blinked at the floor, feeling defeated.

"I'm sorry," he muttered, shaking his head.

"It's okay. There's nothing to apologize for," his matter-of-fact physical therapist, Olivia, said as she made another note on her clipboard. "Let's call it a day, shall we? You made great progress since last time."

"I never thought I'd be so pleased to hear feedback on my walking skills," Andrew tried to joke. "Not since I was a toddler, at least."

Olivia chuckled as she assisted him back to his wheelchair.

"Walking isn't as easy as it looks. We have to trick your muscles into remembering the process is all. I think you'll be back up on your feet with crutches in a little more than three weeks, if you can believe it."

Andrew hardly could.

It had been a little over a month since the accident. He and several soldiers had surrounded an abandoned hospital in Baghdad. Someone had given the all-clear, but they'd missed the bomb waiting in a shadowy entrance. After the ear-splitting explosion, Andrew had collapsed, numb and bleary. When he had blinked down, his right leg had seemed to be nothing but shrapnel and blood.

He was lucky to be alive. He was lucky that he could learn to walk again. Most of the others weren't so lucky and hadn't made it.

He didn't necessarily like to think about that, though.

A van took him back to the ground-floor apartment he had rented in Boston. As he wheeled across the sidewalk, he turned to look down the beautiful street of a city he'd once felt was the pinnacle of all life. Now, however, it was littered with trash and beer bottles. With a jolt, he remembered: the previous night had been St. Patrick's Day, arguably one of the wildest and most outrageous nights in Boston year-round.

Andrew, on the other hand, had taken a sleeping pill and his pain medicine; he'd conked out just after eight-thirty and hadn't heard a thing.

It was March and chillier than ever, but with a friendly little sun poking its head out from beneath a fluffy springtime cloud. Andrew leaned his head back in his chair. He would never return to the Middle East; he would never again be an acting soldier. What would he do with the rest of his life now? Just retire?

It was one of the strangest years of Andrew's life. A few months later, he celebrated his thirty-fifth birthday at the bar alone with crutches on either side of his stool and a glass of whiskey in hand. A woman several stools away gave him a once over with her eyes and asked, "Did you see action?"

"No," he answered. "I was hit by a car."

What was it about the way he looked? Did he just reek of war?

He detested his little ground-floor apartment. He never bothered to trade out the furniture it had come with for furniture he might have liked. The only personal decorations he had bothered with was a framed portrait of him and Kurt on the evening of their graduation and one from them sitting in a bunker a few nights before Kurt had been killed. They were completely suited up in their gear and artillery with wide smiles plastered on their faces. They had both looked like they were untouchable back then. He thought back to that night when he had punched Mike in the face and all the chaos that had followed afterward— after his life had changed for good.

Had Kelli stayed with Mike? Had things calmed down between them? Had their dad been right about keeping out of it? Andrew would never know.

Before Andrew knew what to do with himself or how to mark the calendar of his passing life, it was suddenly Thanksgiving.

Previous Thanksgivings had been almost pleasant. Andrew had been stationed abroad somewhere with his fellow soldiers, all of whom took it upon themselves to craft up a half-decent meal and enough booze to go around for everyone. They had sung songs into the night, swapped stories, and eaten their fair share. There was something about eating Thanksgiving while you were also hard at work serving your country. It was like all the meals across the great United States of America were eaten as a way to honor your service and those who served before you.

The Thanksgiving after he was injured, Andrew ordered

Chinese food and watched football on his television screen. He didn't say a single word, not even to the delivery driver when he slipped him a tip. When he went to bed that night, he wondered if it was possible for a throat to close up due to lack of use.

It was now heading into December. He couldn't believe that eleven months had already passed since he had been released from duty due to his leg injury. Andrew hovered over the magazine and candy bar section at the grocery store. He always gave himself extra time to think about it. Did he want a *Sports Illustrated* and a Twix bar, or a *Time* and a Reese's? This was about as much excitement as his life had these days. As he scanned, his eyes hovered over the wedding section, where two celebrities peered out with wide smiles.

The Most Expensive Martha's Vineyard Wedding Ever. Read about the Wedding Planner Who Made it Happen: Charlotte Hamner

Andrew's hand shook as he lifted the magazine off the rack. The woman beside him in line looked at him, incredulous, shocked that he had picked up a wedding magazine. By the time he reached Charlotte's page, his eyes were so bleary that he couldn't read the words. He bought the magazine, a Twix bar and a Reese's. By the time he arrived back to his couch, he had the energy to read.

It was just a fluff piece, hardly anything: mostly information about the flowers (all done up by Claire Whalen, the wedding planner's sister, his sister), the decorations, and the fact that the bride and groom had called off the wedding for a full five hours before they had decided to go ahead with it at a nearby chapel.

Andrew stopped breathing for a moment. Although there weren't any photos of the chapel, he knew exactly the one they had gone to. They had frequented that place for church services for a few years, and he had fond memories of the soft light in the space, the way the Bibles felt in his hands, and reading the passages that seemed to matter so much to a young, sensitive heart like his.

"I have to give a lot of credit to my daughter, Rachel," Charlotte said in the article. "She's only fourteen, but she kept me together every step of the way. Sometimes I asked myself, who's mothering whom, you know?"

Of course, Andrew had imagined Charlotte had had children. The fact that this daughter was written about so plainly here in a magazine he'd picked up from the grocery store chilled him. He should have learned this fourteen years ago. It almost felt like a calling.

* * *

Andrew wasn't sure if he believed in fate. Actually, if anything, his previous years at war, in the Middle East, or in washed-up apartments in Boston had taught him that there was nothing to this life at all. You were born, you lived, and then you died. That was that.

But the very night he read the article about Charlotte's wedding planning on the Vineyard, his phone rang deep in the night. It had been so long since anyone had called him that he hardly dared answer it.

The Martha's Vineyard area code—508—was the only reason he did.

His voice faltered. "Hello?"

It seemed likely that there would be a ghost on the other end of the line.

There was silence for a long stretch. Andrew lifted his phone from his ear and prepared to hang up. Maybe it was a prank call from the great beyond. Heck, maybe it was even Kurt. They'd loved to prank phone call people, back in the day.

Finally, a voice called out, "Andy? Andy, is that really you?"

Every person who wasn't a Montgomery or a Sheridan had a lot of trouble differentiating between the Montgomery sisters' voices. If anyone else had been listening, they might have thought this was Kelli or even Charlotte.

Andrew's ears knew it instantly, though.

This was Claire.

But how in the heck could he answer? His heart raced a million miles a minute. He ran his fingers through his hair and finally answered, "It's me, Claire. It's me."

Again, there was silence. What could two siblings say to one another after seventeen years apart?

"I wasn't sure if this would be the right number," Claire finally said. "Previous numbers the army has given me over the years always ended up disconnected."

"I guess I never stuck around Boston long enough for any of the numbers to hold up," he told her. "I was always switching SIM cards."

"Wow. Andy." Her voice cracked with emotion. "I wish I was calling you under better circumstances."

Andrew furrowed his brow. After another long pause, he said, "Do I even want to know?"

"None of us want to know this," she whispered. "It happened this afternoon. We got a good deal of snow here, and then this week, it just kept piling on. We're all used to driving in it, or at least, we tell ourselves we're used to it. But Dad, he's getting up there in years. He—"

Again, her voice cracked. Andrew's eyes closed with the heaviness of it all. Suddenly, time had sped up, and he wasn't Claire's kid-brother anymore. Suddenly, she was in her late thirties, and their father was, well—whatever he was. Maybe he was dead.

"He crashed his car into a tree, Andy," Claire said. She full-on sobbed into the phone now. "I don't know why he went out like that. The roads weren't clear and Mom said she needed milk and... Well, you know how Dad is. He's so damn stubborn."

Andrew splayed his hand across his forehead as his shoulders dropped. As he sat there, a smell clouded around him: proof that he hadn't bothered to shower that day. Maybe he'd forgotten the day before, too. He couldn't remember.

"Is he still alive?" Andrew asked. He was fully aware of how cold his words sounded, even in his fear.

"He's hanging on by a thread," Claire whispered. "The doctors are doing everything they can. I left the hospital about an hour ago to take care of my girls and try to get ahold of you."

Her girls. She has girls. I don't know a thing about her girls, my nieces. Not their names or their ages or what they even look like.

"Thank you for calling me," Andrew said somberly.

"Andy, come on. He's your dad. I had to let you know."

They held the silence again. Andrew's head felt like a drum. Memories rushed through his mind: beautiful Claire teasing him from the front of his mother's car while he played with toys in the backseat. Funny Claire, dotting a kiss on his nose when he was still crawling. Claire, who had now reached out to him after seventeen years.

"Just keep me in the loop, I guess," Andrew said somberly. He felt like a used-up Kleenex.

"Andy, I'm calling you because... Well. I think it's time you came home. The army said you've been back in Boston for over eleven months and have no plans of heading back to the Middle East. I don't know what your life is like now. I don't know if you have a girlfriend? A wife? Kids of your own?"

The words were like punches to the gut.

"Regardless of what you've done or what's happened to

you, the entire Montgomery family wants to see you. Even Dad, if he ever—"

If he ever wakes up again.

If he lives through this.

Claire couldn't finish what she'd started. Andrew fidgeted. He told himself to hang up the phone; he told himself that this was nothing but a head-first dive into devastation. He had promised himself a long, long time ago that he wouldn't go back there. He wasn't a Montgomery any longer. His father had made it crystal clear that he didn't belong.

"Please, Andy," Claire whispered. She was fully weeping now, the kind of tears nobody—not even a limping veteran with a heart of black could ignore. "Since you left, it's not like we've forgotten about you. Charlotte and I talk about you all the time. We hate that our girls don't know their Uncle Andy. We hate that we don't know a single thing about your life. Whatever it was that Dad said, I'm sure he regrets it now. He's much softer than he used to be. His career nearly destroyed him; we all know that."

Andrew sighed again. *The old man doesn't deserve my forgiveness. I pledged that I would never see his face again.*

"Andy, the Sheridan sisters came back," Claire said finally. "They forgave Wes. They've begun to heal. When I look at them, I ask myself, why not us? Why can't the Montgomery family find a way back to the old days? Why can't we have that? We need you here, Andy. On the Vineyard. We've never needed you more than we do right now. We miss and love you so much."

Chapter Six

December in Boston was unforgiving in its frigidity. Glittering Christmas lights lined the streets; tinsel advertised various computers and Playstations and brand-new smartphones in the window of the nearby tech store: only $799.99! Andrew hovered outside his old car, the one he had bought second-hand when he had finally gotten the hang of walking again. He jangled his keys as soft snow speckled across his nose and cheeks. Was he really going to do this?

Martha's Vineyard. It awaited him. It felt like a haunted house, its ghosts gazing out at him through the windows, calling for him to return.

As he drove from Boston to Falmouth, his eyes scanned the barren landscape on either side of the highway. He remembered the older guy who had picked him and Kurt up when they'd snuck off the island at age eighteen. Back then, they'd been so vibrant with ideas of what they wanted their lives to be. Had the guy really been that old? Maybe Andrew himself looked a lot like him now. Maybe, if he picked up a hitchhiker now, that kid would look at him the same way Andrew had looked at his driver back then. Of course, nobody was out hunting for a ride, not in that freezing air. With the rise of the internet, people didn't tend to hitchhike any longer, anyway. There were too many articles written about the danger of it all.

Andrew knew where to park his car for free near the ferry dock in Woods Hole. He was surprised that he drove the car there so easily, his hands guiding the steering wheel without any kind of demand on his mind. After all the continents he had marched across, he still remembered.

He bought a ferry ticket and stomped his snowy boots down to the lower deck, where he grabbed a burnt cup of coffee and a muffin from the little café stand. He nibbled at the top of the muffin and let the hot liquid billow out across his tongue. He hadn't tasted anything as good as his mother's cooking in a very long time.

Only a few other people joined him on the ferry. Martha's Vineyard generally closed-up shop in December; people took to their fireplaces, spent time with family, and turned away from the frantic tourist season. He stared straight ahead as he continued to nibble at his muffin. The ferry motor started up beneath them as the boat tore away from the dock.

A woman sat toward the far end of the ferry. Her brunette locks swept down her shoulders; her skin was sun-kissed and her brows were lowered in concentration as she read a large book. Occasionally, she lifted her fingers and nibbled nervously at her nails. Something about her screamed out to Andrew. Something told him she was—

"Charlotte?"

The word tumbled out of his lips. Maybe, if he hadn't been so shocked, he would have found a better tactic to announce himself. That said, she instantly lifted her chin, turned her gorgeous eyes into his, and dropped her book on the ground in utter shock.

There was nothing like this reunion. Andrew abandoned his muffin and coffee and backpack and tore down the aisle, only limping the slightest bit. Charlotte rose to throw her arms around him. As they held one another, Andrew shook with sorrow and fear. Somehow, he wanted to say he was sorry, but he didn't know how to begin.

They stood like that for a few minutes, not letting each go. Their hug finally broke as Charlotte gripped Andrew's shoulders. They studied one another's faces. If Andrew's calculation was correct, Charlotte was forty-one years old and still every bit the beauty she had once been, but her eyes were tired, with big hollow circles beneath them. It was clear she had been crying.

"Oh, Andy. You must think I've gotten so old," Charlotte said suddenly. She splayed her hand across her cheek and exhaled with laughter.

Andrew joined her with a chuckle of his own. "I was just thinking the same thing about me."

"You're thirty-five, aren't you?"

"And you're forty-one."

"It's terrible, isn't it?"

"It really is," Andrew affirmed.

"Come on, sit me with," Charlotte said as she hurriedly shoved her suitcase to the side. "Claire mentioned she finally got ahold of you, but I had my doubts you'd actually..." She stuttered, seemed to think better of her words, then gripped his hand as she added, "I'm so glad you came. I haven't slept a wink since I found out what happened to Dad, so it's possible that you're some kind of waking dream. If you are, you're the best dream I've had in a very long time."

"I'm no dream," Andrew said as he sat beside her. "More of a walking nightmare."

Charlotte's eyes were glassy with tears. Andrew was grateful that none of them fell. The air around them was so taut, like a bubble on the verge of popping. He gestured toward the suitcase and said, "Where are you coming from, anyway? I thought you still lived on the Vineyard."

"I do. None of us left except you and the Sheridan sisters," Charlotte said.

"Claire said they returned."

"Just this past summer," Charlotte affirmed. "They're better than ever. Susan had a pretty bad health scare, but she's through the woods now. They just helped me through the craziest wedding ever. Actually, it's kind of a boring story now."

Andrew had read every inch of the article about it in that silly wedding magazine, but he didn't want to give himself away. "I guess you're a wedding planner?"

"Guilty as charged," Charlotte said, holding her hands up in a joking manner.

"You were always the romantic one, I guess," Andrew said.

"To a fault, some would say," Charlotte affirmed. She shook her head delicately as she added, "I guess I haven't seen you since, what? A week after your graduation? Two weeks? You didn't waste any time."

"Kurt and I got out of here as quickly as we could," Andrew said softly. "And then, not long after that, everything changed."

Charlotte nodded delicately. "I went to his funeral. It was horrible, knowing you were still over there." She closed her eyes as she added, "I guess I should say I was pretty sure you still were over there. You never joined social media or anything, so I never really knew."

Andrew tapped his right leg and said, "Eleven months back with a bum leg. They wouldn't let me tour again even if I wanted to."

All the color drained from Charlotte's face. She gripped his hand and said, "I'm just so glad you're okay."

Andrew was overwhelmed with emotion again. Between the hug and the hand-holding, this was much more physical contact than he'd had in a while. Finally, he forced himself to say, "Seems to me that you're avoiding the question. Where are you coming from?" He tried a smile.

Charlotte lifted her eyebrows. "Right! Right. Um. I'm actually coming back from California right now. Los Angeles."

"Wow. I noticed you looked tanned and refreshed," Andrew said. "What's out there? Was it something for another wedding?"

"Kind of," Charlotte said doubtfully.

"I can't believe you went out to California without Jason," Andrew said. "He must be crazy jealous. But I guess all those fish can't catch themselves."

Charlotte pressed her top teeth into her bottom lip. Again, her eyes filled with tears and threatened to spill over onto her cheeks. Andrew's already fake smile fell off his face. He knew he had said something wrong; he just couldn't figure out what.

"You've been gone so, so long," Charlotte whispered. "You missed so much."

Charlotte turned her eyes toward the ground. The boat rocked slightly with the waves from the Vineyard Sound. Andrew felt as though he could have melted into the chair.

The ferry arrived at the dock in Oak Bluffs before either of them had a chance to clamber back into a proper conversation. Andrew got the hint: Jason wasn't around anymore. But he couldn't fully envision what had happened. Had he left Charlotte? Had they gotten a divorce? What? It felt too strange to ask his sister such an intimate question, especially when he should have been around to already know.

"Claire's here to pick us up," Charlotte announced. She tried a smile that grew bigger as they collected their things. "We'll catch up. We'll find the time now that you're back. I'm sure this is all a lot to deal with right now, but just know we have your back every step of the way." Charlotte reached up and touched his cheek. "We've missed you so much, Andrew."

Chapter Seven

"Baby, look at your fingers! They're so sticky!" Beth Leopold knelt at the kitchen table before her eight-year-old son, Will, and dabbed at his fingers with a wet cloth. Will stuck out his bottom lip and said, "I'm not done with my Pop-Tart yet."

Beth glanced at the blueberry Pop-Tart he'd torn apart; it was scattered across his plate and over his lap. The guts of it had made his fingers a godforsaken mess, and he hadn't bothered to touch his oatmeal.

"Eat four bites of oatmeal, and then you can finish your Pop-Tart," she said.

Will's eyes looked empty and tired. The previous days had been difficult for him. He hadn't managed to make it to school. Beth had had to take time off to calm him down, sit with him and stroke his hair and tell him everything would be all right very soon.

Every time the school called Beth with another report of "Will can't seem to handle the other kids today," or "Will can't stop crying," her heart took on yet another bruise. As a mother of an autistic child, she sometimes felt on the verge of collapse. His fears and anxieties were like shadows that chased after both of them. Just when they settled into some kind of routine, the shadows darkened with newfound fears.

Will was an adorable kid. He had shaggy black hair, which she had cut into a bowl, and his eyes were round and the color of the Vineyard Sound itself. His lips were bowtie-shaped and light pink, and as he chewed his oatmeal, he was careful to chew softly and with his mouth closed, as she'd taught him. Her heart surged with love.

"Will, can I ask you something?"

Will swallowed his oatmeal and said, "Yes, Mommy. You can."

"Do you think you can handle school today?"

Will contemplated this for a long time. He'd never lied in his life, something that made him one of the better creatures on this earth. That said, it sometimes took him some time to deduce precisely how he felt.

"I think I can," Will said. "I really do."

After breakfast, Beth tucked Will into the backseat of her car. He was all bundled up with a soft yellow hat and bright blue mittens and a winter coat she had gotten as a hand-me-down from the neighbors. He sang softly to himself as she buckled him in. Only when she sat down in the front seat did she realize the full brevity of her fatigue. She had hardly slept a wink the previous nights, as she'd been so worried about Will's tumultuous emotions.

Beth had never been the type of woman to blame others for the mixed-up nature of her life. Will's autism was a fact of life and often a blessing. She firmly believed that all blessings had their own shades of darkness. He was the lasting product of a summertime fling nine years before when she had been twenty-five years old and still reeling from the death of her brother, Kurt. If she was honest about that, she was still reeling from the death of her brother. Since then, of course, she'd also had to add on the deaths of both of her parents. She was now an orphan and the only one left in her family, besides Will, of course.

Will was excited about Christmas in a way that seemed to minimize any other child's excitement about the holiday. As she drove to his elementary school, he gabbed about Santa as though the two were old pals. By the time they reached the drop-off area, Will had made up his mind to write yet another letter to the old man in the North Pole, just in case the other letters hadn't made it through. Beth made a mental note to fake a letter back from Santa; Will needed some affirmation.

But wasn't that a lie? Was it wrong to lie to a little boy who couldn't fully comprehend the concept of a lie?

Beth kissed her son and wished him good luck. As he walked into the elementary school alongside the other boys and girls, she prayed he would have a better day—no freak-outs. No crying. No thinking that everyone was after him.

Beth drove the rest of the way to the hospital, parked, and darted into the crisp white hallways. After graduation, she had gone off to university to become a registered nurse. Over the years, she had worked in many different departments in several nursing capacities. These days, she mostly focused on rehabilitation, although she occasionally took rounds in the ER when things were slow.

Beth's best friend stood in the break room with a clipboard in hand. She wore light pink scrubs and little Christmas tree earrings, a gift from her daughter.

"Ellen!" Beth said as she entered the room and yanked off her winter coat.

"There you are. I was worried you wouldn't make it in today," Ellen said with a genuine smile.

"Will seemed ready today," Beth said. "More focused and a part of the world. I hope it holds."

"The kid's strong," Ellen affirmed. "It's the other kids that throw him off."

"I know you're right," Beth said. "How's it going in the ER this week? I haven't paid much attention."

"Actually, we had a pretty bad accident yesterday afternoon," Ellen said as she tapped the clipboard back in place atop the metal cabinet beside her. "Trevor Montgomery."

Beth's heart sank. She'd known the old real estate mogul for decades; his son had run off to war with Kurt and never returned.

"Oh, no. How's he doing?" *Please don't say he's dead. Please don't say he's dead.*

"Haven't had time to check up on him today, but the other nurses said it's been touch and go since he arrived," Ellen explained. "He ran into a tree."

"The snow," Beth breathed. "It can make some of these roads so dangerous at times." Her heart sank into her stomach and thudded softly. "You'll let me know how it goes?"

"Of course," Ellen affirmed. Her eyes were hollow as she added, "I guess they don't have high expectations. He's up there in age these days."

"The body can't take a beating like that very well. I know," Beth said sadly.

* * *

Beth went through the motions of her early shift. Her arms and legs felt heavy as lead as she assisted an older woman who'd had a stroke and needed to regain use of her arm. She helped a little boy with inappropriate walking patterns and then spoke with a middle-aged mother with multiple sclerosis about the approaching years, how her motions would change, and what she could do to fight it.

All the while, a portion of her subconscious thought about Trevor Montgomery.

When she took her lunch break, she nibbled at the edge of a carrot stick and thought back to the last time she had ever seen her brother, Kurt, alive. She had driven Kurt and Andrew up to Boston to that cockroach-infested apartment they'd called their "bachelor pad," or whatever. Thinking back now, she had always had a crush on Andrew; it had pained her to think that he wanted to live somewhere else, away from the island. Still, in her heart of hearts, she had always believed that he and Kurt would return to the Vineyard. Everyone always came back. No matter how complicated it got with family, no matter how dark the memories got, they returned.

She hadn't banked on them signing up for the army, though.

During that first year they had spent in Afghanistan, Beth had run into Mr. and Mrs. Montgomery only a handful of times. Back then, they'd been some of the richest people on the island, rubbing elbows with celebrities and top-notch NYC journalists and even a few politicians. Still, when they spotted her, their eyes would cloud up with the shared memory of Andrew. Worry permeated across their foreheads, even as they smiled and said, "Hello there."

They had gone to Kurt's funeral to pay their respects. In Oak Bluffs, everyone knew everyone else, and devastation had filled the nooks and crannies of the town, so much so that the outpouring of love and support in the wake of Kurt's death had been almost overwhelming. Beth had blocked out a lot of that time of her life. Maybe Kerry Montgomery had offered a kind word; maybe Trevor Montgomery had given her a hug or a smile. Nothing anybody did had helped at all. Her brother had been her favorite person in the world—her best friend. When he was gone, a part of her died along with him.

For the record, Trevor and Kerry had gone to Beth's

parents' funerals as well. Of course they had. All of Oak Bluffs had, too.

Although she still had twenty minutes left of her break, Beth dropped her carrot stick back in its plastic baggie and zipped it up before she shoved it back in the lunchbox. Guided by an invisible force, she found her way toward inpatient care, where she knew Trevor Montgomery's white and sterile hospital bed held him hostage.

Beth stood outside the closed door with her hands clenched at her sides. She wasn't sure what she'd expected to find; the man was in a coma and there wasn't anything to be done other than wait. The door swung open to reveal—of all people—her best friend, Ellen, who'd taken those rounds that day. She remained jotting something on her clipboard with the door open, which allowed Beth a small peek into the room.

"Oh, Beth! Hey," Ellen said as the door closed behind her. "I didn't expect to see you here."

Beth crossed and uncrossed her arms. "How's he doing?"

"No change, I'm afraid," Ellen said. "Kerry's in there fast asleep. I wanted to grab her a pillow and a blanket to keep her warm."

"Won't you let me do it?" Beth asked softly. "Me and the Montgomerys go way back."

"Okay. Thank you, Beth." Ellen started to walk away as she added, "But you shouldn't be working on your lunch break. You know better. I don't want you to run yourself ragged again."

Beth found the spare pillows and blankets in the nearby breakroom, which doctors and nurses occasionally used to take naps in the middle of overly-long shifts. When she returned to the hospital room, she gently pushed the door open as quietly as she could and stepped within to find Trevor Montgomery: all seventy-some years of him. His head was wrapped up in fresh and bright white bandages, as were his left arm and his left leg. One of his fingers on his right hand seemed to be broken as well and had been taped to stay totally flat. His lips looked chapped, as though they'd only just stopped bleeding.

The sight nearly took Beth's breath away.

On the other side of the bed was his loving wife, Kerry Montgomery. According to Andrew, the pair had been high school sweethearts, as was traditional on this island. In their mid-twenties, they had gone on to have the first of their five children. The rest, as they said, was history.

The blanket fluttered over Kerry's legs, which she had stretched out on a spare chair in front of her. She slept beautifully, like a lady, so unlike the way Beth had slept the few times Will had had to stay overnight in the hospital. Each time she had woken up, she'd found spittle all across her makeshift pillow.

Beth left the pillow next to Kerry for her to find. She wasn't sure how to prop it under her without waking her.

That moment, the door cracked open. She hadn't expected Ellen back so soon. She whirled around to discover not only Ellen but Wes Sheridan, Kerry's brother, along with Susan Sheridan, Wes's eldest daughter. Beth had heard recently about Susan's cancer diagnosis; at this stage after chemotherapy, most of her hair had grown back. The shortness of it actually highlighted the beauty of her cheekbones, the stunning light of her eyes, and the youthfulness of her skin. Everyone in the world had always been envious of the Sheridan sisters. Although Beth had been quite a bit younger than even their youngest, Lola, even she had felt the adoration the entire island had. When they returned home, it had felt like an earthquake had shaken their little island.

Wes and Susan's eyes turned from the sleeping Kerry up toward Beth, the nurse. There was no reason on the planet that they should have recognized her, which meant the "Beth! Hello!" that Susan whispered surprised Beth a great deal.

"Hello!" she hissed back with a smile.

"Thanks for taking such good care of my uncle," Susan said as she stepped forward and squeezed her shoulder in a tender way. "We've been so worried about him, but knowing he's in your trustworthy hands is such a Godsend."

"Actually, I'm not his on-duty nurse," Beth explained. "My friend is. I just came in to give your Aunt Kerry a pillow and blanket. I know how hard on the body these long days and nights can be when you don't have a bed of your own."

"The old girl won't leave his side," Wes said. He dropped in the free chair beside his sister's head and stared down at his shoes.

There was something about his manner, something lost about his eyes.

Had Beth missed something? Did old Wes Sheridan have a condition that hadn't been announced?

"Even still, the fact that you're watching out for them is so kind," Susan said. "Needless to say, none of us has gotten much sleep since it happened. My sisters begged to come along to say hello, but there really isn't a need for them in this room. Not till he wakes up, at least."

If he wakes up.

That moment, Kerry Montgomery's eyes opened softly, like a flower opening shyly at the beginning of spring. She blinked, looking confused as her eyes focused on Beth. "Nurse?" she said as she shifted up and dropped her feet to the ground. "Nurse, I wondered, is he getting enough fluids?"

"This isn't his nurse, Aunt Kerry," Susan said. "This is Beth Leopold. You must remember her."

Kerry blinked several more times before she dropped her chin to her chest. Guilt seemed to permeate across her face. Beth wanted to reach out, grab her hand, and tell her all of it. The pain they had all experienced wasn't really anyone's fault. It was just what life was.

"Beth. It's good to see you," Kerry whispered. She looked at her like Beth was a ghost. "Goodness, I suppose I forgot you worked here."

Beth swallowed the lump in her throat as she said, "There's a pillow here beside you, just in case you need it later."

"Seems to me Trevor and I have some visitors," Kerry said. The color began to return to her face. She gave Wes a smile and grabbed his hand. "Good thing, too. I'll have to send you guys to the vending machine."

Wes chuckled as Susan rolled her eyes playfully. "The woman hasn't eaten anything but healthy home-cooked food for fifty years. What does she think vending machines are stocked with? Kale salads?"

Beth laughed in spite of it all, her fingers touching her lips as she smiled. Susan walked over to sit by her Aunt Kerry. Slowly, their conversation folded into itself, like dough stretched over a pie, already hidden away, no longer inclusive of Beth. Beth said goodbye to them, and they said their thanks. Softly, she slipped back out the door, walked toward the break-room where she knew it would be quiet, and soon found herself in a heap in the corner with tears rolling toward her chin. So much had happened over the years, but just because so much already had, didn't mean that any of them was safe from heartache.

Chapter Eight

Since Charlotte had said, "You've missed so much," to Andrew on the ferry boat, they hadn't managed many words to one another. They stood out on the dock, with Charlotte's suitcase in front of them and Andrew's military duffel bag flung over his shoulder. Snow fluttered around them, just as beautiful as any Christmas card, as Andrew acknowledged the world he'd once given up on. There it was: the magnificent Oak Bluffs— now transformed for Christmas. There was holly lining the streets, each tree decorated with bulbs and lights, and that old, familiar, terribly historical carousel twinkling in the distance. It looked like a picture out of a Christmas card. It was so magical.

"I'm sorry," Charlotte interjected suddenly.

Andrew arched his brow. "What do you mean?"

"I mean, I didn't mean to say that you've missed so much. I'm sure you've been through so much of your own chaos. I never want to make you feel guilty."

Andrew nodded somberly. He wanted to say a million things, like, *I've thought about you, Kelli, Claire, and Steven every single day since I left. I've missed you terribly. When I first read about your daughter, Rachel, I nearly wept.*

But some things were better off not said, maybe. Or maybe he just wasn't the sort of guy capable of saying them.

He was like his father in that way, which to him felt like he had been tainted.

Before Andrew had the chance to answer, there was a loud honk of a horn. He searched the sea of vehicles to find a little blue car with one Claire Montgomery standing out of the driver's seat and waving a long arm to alert them. Her smile was electric.

"That's our Claire," Charlotte laughed. "She always likes to lighten the mood. However, you should have seen her while we put that wedding together. I would catch her crying in every corner. I wasn't sure any of us would make it out of that alive."

"But you did," Andrew said as they headed toward the car. He tried his hardest not to limp at all, which was a struggle with every step. Probably, Charlotte had noticed and had decided not to mention it. That was always her way.

"We did. We'll have to tell you more about it when there's time," Charlotte said. "I'm still reeling from all the emotion of it. It was like a marathon, but we had to sprint the whole thing."

At the car, Claire whipped around and barreled her athletic body into Andrew's in only the kind of hug an older sister could give a younger brother. She screeched and gripped him as hard as she could. Andrew was surprised to feel his heart grow just the slightest bit warmer.

"Look at you," Claire breathed as she fell back. "You look—"

"Like an old man?" Andrew interjected.

"Not in the least," Claire said. "I was going to say, like a young and scruffy Brad Pitt."

Andrew rolled his eyes, even as the sides of his mouth ticked upward into a smile.

"Look at him. There's that smile I remember so well," Claire teased. "Charlotte, you see it, don't you?"

Charlotte's eyes were a tad cloudy. She'd felt the sadness that fell from Andrew.

"He's our little brother all right, through and through," Charlotte said.

Charlotte then turned around to wave into the backseat of the car, where two identical teenage girls sat. They peered curiously at their Uncle Andrew with faces that reminded Andrew so much of both Charlotte and Claire when they'd been teenagers.

Claire rapped at the window and called, "Girls! Come out here and meet your Uncle Andy."

Andrew stood like a statue as the girls barreled out of the car and stood side-by-side to blink up at him.

"Andy, these are my girls, Gail and Abby," Claire announced. "They turned fifteen this past July. And girls, this is your Uncle Andy, who you've heard so much about over the years."

"Hello, Uncle Andy," one of them said.

"Hey," the other said.

Andrew had no idea which one was which.

The one on the left gasped, yanked open the car door, then reappeared with a bouquet of marigolds. She pressed them into Andrew's hands and said, "We made this for you."

Andrew's heart fell into his stomach. The smell of the flowers overwhelmed him. Through his years as a bachelor, he hadn't so much as purchased a single candle.

"Thank you, Gail and Abby," he said softly. "It's wonderful to meet you." He made eye contact with each of them. He wanted them to know how much it meant.

"The girls are wonderful with flowers," Claire affirmed. "Seems to me they're even better than I was when I started the flower shop. You remember that Andy, right? When I made you help me set up all those cabinets and the front counter?"

"How could I forget?" Andrew said with his first real smile. "You hardly had two pennies to rub together."

"Things are a little bit different now," Claire said.

Silence fell over them as the snow picked up. Andrew shivered slightly as Gail and Abby exchanged glances. Finally, Claire insisted that they all pile in the car so they could drop off their stuff and head up to the hospital.

Everything about the drive felt sinister to Andrew. It all seemed the same but different: the same houses with different people living in them; the same restaurants with different names. On the way to the house he'd grown up in, they stopped briefly at Charlotte's, where apparently, their cousin, Christine and her boyfriend, Zach, had stayed while Charlotte had run off to California. She dropped off her suitcase and spoke with Christine on the front porch. Christine waved a hand to the car, and Gail, Abby, and Claire all waved back. Andrew couldn't do it. He hadn't seen Christine since he'd been something like ten or eleven years old. She was basically a stranger to him now.

When Charlotte got back into the passenger seat, she said, "Christine reports that Rachel was on her best behavior while I was away. I think she missed you girls at school today, though."

"We've all just been so sick to our stomachs about Grandpa, haven't we? I couldn't make them go to school," Claire explained.

A few moments later, one of the twins said, "How was California, Aunt Charlotte?"

"And Everett! How was he?" the other asked.

Charlotte turned toward the back, where Andrew sat on the left, with the two girls beside him. "It was a dream come true," she said. "Everett showed me all his favorite spots in LA, and we went to the beach three times."

"He's so handsome," one of the twins said.

"Gail!" the other one said.

The one in the middle is Abby; the one on this end is Gail. Got it. Maybe.

Charlotte laughed good-naturedly. "He's a keeper for sure. I think he might try to come out here for Christmas. He fell in love with the island."

"He loved a little more than the island," Claire teased.

Did Jason leave her? Did they get divorced? Where is Jason?

Andrew couldn't breathe when he first spotted his house for the first time: that three-story old-world beauty that was built in 1880 and restored when his parents had latched onto more money than they had known what to do with. It had always been blue, a glorious dark-sky-blue, and the shutters were dark gray. If Andrew hadn't been fully aware of the pain in his right leg and his heart, he might have felt he'd just stepped back in time.

"Here we are," Claire said. She glanced into the rearview to catch Andrew's eye as she said, "Nothing much different about it, huh, Andy?"

Andrew shook his head. "Not at all."

Andrew escaped the tightness of the backseat a bit too quickly and landed hard on his bad leg. He winced just as Claire got out of the car and caught him. Her eyes scanned down to his leg, but she didn't say a thing.

"Let's get you inside. You must be exhausted and starving," she said.

Older sister, younger brother alert.

His mother had updated the interior quite a bit since 2003. There was a new couch in the living area, a new-to-them antique table in the dining room, and updated photographs of the grand-children scattered around the house. An old photograph of Kerry and her brother, Wes, hung in the kitchen, and an old photograph of the Sheridan clan before Aunt Anna had died sat on the piano.

Andrew's heart hammered in his throat as he dropped his duffel bag to his side and ogled it all. The nostalgia was so overwhelming that he had to swallow the lump that had formed in his throat.

"Have any idea where I'm supposed to stay?" he asked Claire.

"I don't think they've done much to your bedroom," she said without making eye contact. "You can make yourself comfortable there if you like."

Andrew's eyes traveled up the length of the staircase as he made his way to his room.

It was like entering a tomb.

Andrew stood in a somber reflection in the old bedroom, the one he'd taken over after Steven had left the house and married Laura. His Blink-182 poster still hung over his bed; a photo of him and Kurt near the baseball diamonds still sat on his dresser; his bed was made up in fresh sheets and a comforter, as though his mother had expected him to return home any time.

His leg gave out on him, and he collapsed on the edge of the bed. He massaged the area just beneath his knee and tried to stop the ringing in his ears.

You're okay. You're still here. You're going to get through this.

Downstairs, he heard Claire, Charlotte, Gail, and Abby's murmurs. Were they talking about him? Of course they were; he was the elephant in the room, wasn't he? He was the black sheep of the family—the one who had run away as fast as he could, only to literally limp home seventeen years later.

When Andrew reappeared downstairs, a man who looked nearly fifty years old sat on the brand-new couch. He wore a worn baseball hat, a thick coat fit for skiing, and rugged-looking boots. The television was on in front of him; it showed a rerun basketball game for a local college team.

The girls were in the kitchen, out of sight, if not out of earshot. Andrew stood like a shadow near the staircase and waited for a long moment as the outline of the man's nose, his eyebrows, and his lips formulated a memory of an old-world Steven Montgomery.

If his calculations were correct, his brother was now forty-seven years old.

"Steve?"

The man turned toward the sound. The smile that jumped to his lips was every bit Steve, the brother Andrew had looked up to with adoration and the tiniest bit of envy. He leaped to his feet and extended his arms into a bear hug that required no words. There in Steven's embrace, Andrew felt for the first time like the little Andy he had left behind in the past. It was crippling, even in how beautiful it was.

The hug broke and Steven's arms fell to his sides as he evaluated Andrew. His smile didn't falter, not even once. Steven's heart had always been the purest of the pure.

"It's so good to see you, man," Steven said.

"You too," Andrew said. He was grateful Steven hadn't called him Andy. Maybe he recognized how painful it was for him. "I wish the circumstances were different."

"Me too," Steven said as he adjusted his baseball cap. Even in the rapid motion, Andrew caught that Steven had lost quite a bit of hair. "I spent most of the night at the hospital with Mom. I had to put in a bit of work today. Claire called me this morning and said she'd finally gotten ahold of you. I couldn't believe it."

At that moment, the screen door that led in from the garage slammed shut. Andrew stepped forward to catch sight of another woman—not the family beauties Charlotte and Claire, but an older woman, beautiful in her own right, with eyes filled with sorrow.

The moment Kelli's eyes found his, Andrew's entire right leg spasmed and his heart almost leaped out of his ribcage.

He gasped, gripped his knee, and crumpled against the nearest wall. Steven jumped for him, even as Andrew said, "Don't worry about it. Just a cramp." Kelli walked slowly into the room with worry and sadness marred over her face. Andrew had never wanted to cry his eyes out as hard as he did right then.

"Kelli," he whispered.

That was all he had to say. Kelli rushed toward him and swallowed him in yet another hug, the kind that made his heart stop and his mind pray that he could turn back the clock. Gosh, he'd always loved her so much. He had prayed for her and wanted his fist to end all the problems she'd had all those years ago with Mike.

When she drew back from the hug, he glanced to see that, in fact, she still wore that same damn wedding ring.

"How have you been?" she asked. Her voice rasped.

"I'm good. I've been good," he lied. She could always, always tell when he lied. It was a game they'd played, especially when she'd asked, *Are you drunk again?* Or, *Did you skip class today?* She understood, somehow, that the traditional life that had been okay for all of them wasn't right for him.

She reached up and brushed a few strands of hair from his face. "Do they not have barbers in Boston?"

"They haven't invented them up there yet," he told her.

Kelli's eyes shone with humor. "Remember that time I cut your hair? You were what? Three? Four? I was just Rachel's age, I guess. Fourteen, maybe fifteen. I thought I'd done such a good job, but Mom almost bit my head off."

"I think age three is a little young for much memory," Andrew said. "Although the story's been recounted enough times for me to have made up a memory of my own."

Kelli chuckled. "You were like my little toy doll for those

years. Until one day, you came up to me, covered in mud, and you hugged me as if your life depended on it. I realized in those moments: oh. This kid is not a doll. He's a *boy*."

"Horrible. Boys are horrible," Steven affirmed. "Now that I've raised one of my own, I know the truth. Isabella was a dream compared to Jonathon."

"Wow. How old are they now?" Andrew asked.

"Jonathon's married if you can believe it," he said. "Twenty-four years old with two kids of his own. And Isabella is twenty. She's dated half the island, it feels like. She drives me wild in her own way."

"And you, Kelli? Sam, Josh, and Lexi..."

"I'm surprised you remember all their names," Kelli said softly. "You left when Lexi was just a little baby."

"I remember," Andrew said. "You taught me how to hold her head. Her eyelids were thinner than paper."

A tear rolled down Kelli's cheek then. The emotion between them felt like being in the very center of a horrific storm.

"I can't believe you remember that, either," she confessed.

Charlotte and Claire appeared in the living room. Claire held a platter of Christmas cookies, which she shoved out in front of the other three siblings. "Come on, guys. Gail and Abby have baked and decorated these all day long. We saved some for Grandpa and Grandma up at the hospital, but we need you guys to taste test."

Kelli, Steven, and Andrew all reached in for a Christmas tree or a candy cane or a reindeer-frosted cookie. Andrew tapped his teeth on the outside of his reindeer and was overwhelmed with memories. When all the others had left the house, it had been up to him to help his mother decorate the cookies. They'd had a kind of assembly-line process for it; they'd produced enough for the family and for the Sheridans and for all their neighbors and friends.

"Is this Mom's recipe?" he asked Claire.

"Of course it is," Claire affirmed.

"Delicious, girls," Steven called. "Really. I don't think I've eaten anything all day long. Too nervous."

It was decided that they needed to head up to the hospital. Charlotte mentioned that nobody had had the time or the inclination to tell their mother about Andrew's arrival. "It's too heavy," she whispered to him as he headed toward Steve's truck.

Steve's truck was a 4x4 dark blue monster, with loads of tools from his auto shop in the back. When they were inside the truck together, the smell of the auto shop was almost overwhelming, but in a nostalgic way. All those years ago, Andrew had treasured his brother's ability to make a path for his own future and family. He didn't need to follow the real estate path or whatever life his parents had wanted for him.

"This is a nice truck," Andrew commented.

"Thanks, man," Steven said. "I just got it last year. Laura told me I should treat myself after all the years of hard work. Plus, now that the kids are out of the house, we don't have as many expenses. It's just us. Us and this truck."

Andrew laughed appreciatively as Steven revved the engine. Suddenly, someone placed their hand on the window beside him. When he turned his head, he found Kelli, who called, "Can I ride with you guys?"

Andrew, being the youngest, shoved into the middle of the truck to allow Kelli the passenger seat. She thanked them and breathed into her hands to warm them. Every single time Andrew noticed her looking at him, she looked ready to burst into tears. So for a distraction, he fiddled with the radio and found a song they all loved. It was Nirvana. "Smells Like Teen Spirit."

"I showed this to you the first time," Steven insisted as they drove to the hospital. "You nearly lost your mind."

"I never really got over it," Andrew said with a laugh. "Me and Kurt thought Kurt Cobain was our God."

"He was," Kelli said. "He really was."

* * *

Andrew hadn't been to the hospital since his injury. As he stepped through the double-wide doors, flashbacks of that horrific time came in droves. The early days of bandages and heavy painkillers and the kinds of headaches that felt like throwing a boomerang around his head. They were nothing he wanted to relive.

Now, his father was going through something similar. No, ten times worse.

Kelli, Charlotte, Claire, Steven, Gail, and Abby led Andrew down several hallways, past rooms that made beeping sounds and frantic nurses who hadn't slept enough. With each step that Andrew took, he felt like he was headed toward war again. Once upon a time, he thought he was brave. Now?

Steven glanced at him a few times. His eyes did that little up-down thing as he noticed Andrew's limp. Andrew hated it, but there was nothing to be done. He gave Steven a half-smile and continued until they appeared before a closed-door, one that, presumably, was the final passageway through which they would find their father.

"The five of us. Back together again," Claire whispered.

Suddenly, a nurse opened the door to reveal an overly white room, the tail-end of a bed where some feet pointed upward, and an older woman, just seventy maybe, with her head pressed forward a bit with her eyes closed, as though she was in the middle of prayer.

That moment, as though she knew somewhere in her heart, her eyes flashed up. They found Andrew through the crack in the door. Their eyes locked and suddenly, she moved with the speed and agility of a much younger woman. She tore toward the door, grabbed the handle just as the door began to click shut, and yanked it open just enough to hold her little frame. All the while, her eyes had nowhere else to go but Andrew's.

"Andy?" she breathed. She spoke as though she had walked through a dream. "Andy, is that you?" She took another step closer as her eyes widened and tears rolled down her cheeks. Her fingers pressed against her mouth to contain her shocked gasp.

Her four children who had stayed behind stepped to the side to allow their mother full access to her youngest son. Yet again, her arms reached out to hold onto him, and she drew him tightly against her. Andrew's cheek fell onto her shoulder; he shook slightly as her hand rubbed his upper back, the way it had when he'd had a fever.

"Andy. Andy, my boy," she breathed. "Andy."

The tears were heavy. Once they flowed freely, everyone had tears in their eyes, with some wiping their cheeks with their sleeve as they watched the emotional reunion. On instinct, Andrew laced his arm through his mother's and led her toward a breakroom they had passed on the way. He poured them both a cup of coffee and sat across his mother as her tender eyes continued to study him.

"I never imagined you would be gone so long," she breathed. "And now, look at you. You're a man and so handsome."

Andrew tried his best to keep it together and gave her a small smile. He reached for her hand and gripped it. "I'm here now, Mom."

"You can't leave before your father wakes up," she whispered. Her voice was urgent. "He will want to see you. He needs to know you're all right."

Andrew felt like he had been stabbed. According to what his siblings had told him, there was a good possibility that their father might never wake up. It might be too late to make any of their past heartaches heal.

"I'll stay," he breathed. He needed to say this; it was what she wanted to hear.

"Good," she said. She took a small sip of coffee and grimaced. When she sat it back down, she brought her other hand over his so that she was totally wrapped up in him. "Andy. Andrew. You don't know how long I've dreamed of this. Here you are. And I have so, so many things to say."

At that moment, the breakroom door burst open to reveal Claire. Her cheeks were bright pink and splotchy.

"He's awake. Mom, Andy. He's awake."

Chapter Nine

Seventy-one-year-old Kerry Montgomery moved like a spritely teen from the breakroom. She burst down the hallway, her flats clacking across the linoleum. Far behind her, her youngest son, Andrew, limped forward and winced with every step.

Outside his father's room, the doctor spoke to Kelli, Steven, Claire, Charlotte, Gail, and Abby with soft tones, his forehead shoved forward and his eyebrows lowered. Kerry didn't hesitate to speak with the doctor. She rushed directly through the door, which remained flung open as Andrew neared it. With the door still open, first Steven, then Kelli, then Claire ambled in as well. Their voices rang out like a chorus.

"Dad! You're awake!"

The nurse who remained in the room hissed at them. "I told you guys. Your father can't handle all this at once. It's too much stimulation—"

Kerry hustled to the other side of the bed and leaned down to gently lay a hand over his father's still-broad shoulder as she whispered, "Darling, we're all here for you. Take as much time as you need. We'll postpone Christmas if we need to."

Andrew remained several steps outside the door. He hadn't yet seen his father's face. Just the idea of the old man, there lying immobile in a hospital bed, was enough to chill him to the bone. He was reminded of being a little kid, of thinking his father was the strongest man in the universe. Now, they were both crippled, struck down by the events of their lives.

And Andrew certainly didn't have the strength to enter that room. He hadn't prepared himself. Nobody had alluded that the old man would choose his first day to open his eyes.

"Thank you for heeding the nurse's warnings," the doctor said to him, Gail, and Abby, who remained even further back in the hall with wide, worried eyes, like those of frightened deer. He also grumbled, "I don't know how anyone expects us to run a tight ship around here when they don't pay attention to the rules..." as he marched back within the white room to tell everyone to stand back. "There can be only one visitor in the room at a time! We will let you know when he's strong enough to increase the count."

A shaky voice rang out to the left of Andrew.

"Andy? Is that really you?"

Andrew forced his eyes from the bottom half of his father's hospital bed and turned to find a beautiful woman in her mid-thirties. Her eyes were tender, soft, and her raven hair cascaded like a waterfall down her shoulders and toward her chest. She wore blue nurse's scrubs and scuffed tennis shoes, and she looked at him as though he was some kind of gift.

It had been a long time since anyone had looked at Andrew like that.

It only took a split second for Andrew to realize it was Beth Leopold, Kurt's sister, now standing in front of him. And in the moment of that realization, his heart burst into a million pieces.

"Beth," he breathed.

The corners of her mouth turned upward; her eyes shone with humor and light. "I was worried you wouldn't recognize me. It's been so long. Seventeen years?"

He nodded. There was something about the swoop of her nose, the furrow of her eyebrows. She and Kurt had been only a year apart, Irish twins, and there were certainly similarities, so much so that Andrew could draw out a mental map of what Kurt might have looked like at age thirty-five if he had lived.

If only he had lived.

At that moment, his siblings piled out of the hospital room. They were angry that they'd been kicked out of their father's hospital room yet thrilled to pieces that he'd awoken, especially when the prognosis had been so terrible only a few hours before.

"Nothing can beat that man," Claire said excitedly as tears rolled down her cheeks. "He can take out a tree and wake up the next day as if nothing happened."

Steven smacked his chest with a hand that seemed oiled from his long day at the auto shop. His cheeks were blotched red, but his grin was infectious. He stepped closer to Gail and Abby and said, "He made a joke the second he saw me. He said, 'So, Stevie, what's for dinner?' Can you believe that?"

Gail laughed nervously. Andrew's eyes flashed from Kelli to Steven, then back to Beth. Neither he nor Beth knew what to say. Since his siblings had cleared away from his father, he caught full sight of the old man: the thick bandages around his face and head and his broken arm.

At the hospital in Baghdad, that was all I ever saw. Broken people. People who would never walk again. People who'd given everything for their country. And for what?

"You all right, Andy?" Charlotte said as she stepped toward him. She wrapped an arm around his shoulder, but he'd already begun to shake.

Nothing could stop it: the PTSD attack.

The shaking pushed Andrew back toward the far wall. He placed his hands over his cheeks and blinked several times. He tried to will himself back to the world. *Dad's awake in there. He wants to see you. It's been seventeen years. Seventeen years and enough time to forgive and forget. Pull it together. He doesn't want to see his son all messed up from PTSD. He wants a confident, able son. Don't limp. Don't limp.*

He lost track of everything. He couldn't hear his siblings, couldn't make sense of the white walls or the white linoleum floors. At some points, his mind told him he'd entered some kind of blisteringly light world, a kind of heaven, while at other times, the screeching in his ears told him he'd entered a kind of hell. Sweat pooled along his brow and at the base of his neck.

Maybe it would be better if I wasn't here at all.

* * *

Andrew woke in an unfamiliar vehicle. He blinked into the soft gray light of a beautiful Martha's Vineyard winter late afternoon as snow fluttered down and landed little polka-dots across the windshield. In his hand, he held a water bottle that he didn't recognize. His knees knocked together as he continued to shake.

"That's right, Andy. Just keep breathing." The voice was angelic, like a song.

"Where—where am I?"

"You're in my car," the voice told him. "Just outside the hospital."

"Oh."

Shame fell over him for a moment as he remembered his PTSD attack just outside his father's hospital room.

"I probably freaked out my brother and sisters," he whispered.

"Just a little. They're worried about you. I got you out of there pretty fast," the voice said.

Andrew took a long, cool drink of water and forced himself to turn his head. Somehow, his head felt like the heaviest rock in the world.

Beth Leopold smiled at him from the driver's seat of a little beat-up car. She wore only her scrubs still, despite the chill, and her cheeks had brightened to a shade of crimson that made her impossibly beautiful.

"You got me out of there," Andrew said. His voice remained groggy. "Thank you."

"Don't worry about it," Beth replied.

"It all got a little overwhelming in there," Andrew said. "I guess it's been a pretty chaotic twenty-four hours."

Beth clicked on the radio to an old station from the nineties and early two-thousands, a time period that sizzled with memories of their high school days.

"You have every right to be freaked out," she told him. "Hospitals are emotional places. And I have a hunch you've seen your fair share. They must be a trigger for you."

"I've had my share of hospitals, although I think more to blame is the fact that it's been seventeen years since I've been back," Andrew whispered. "I don't know why I thought this would be okay."

Beth nodded. She reached for her purse slowly and searched through it until she found a package of Oreos, which she handed to him with a firm nod. "You should eat something. Family members of people in the hospital never remember to eat."

"You keep a lot of spare snacks on you?" Andrew asked, trying to lighten the mood as he took the package.

"I have an eight-year-old," Beth affirmed. "Eight-year-olds are constantly hungry."

Andrew tore open the silver and blue packaging and placed

a cookie between his teeth. As he bit down, Beth said, "I see you've become a monster."

Andrew's heart sank. First, she had this whole other life where she had a kid; next, she saw him for what he truly was these days? His eyes were hooded as he searched for what to say.

"I mean, I've never seen you eat an Oreo without taking it apart first," she said. "You just bit down without rhyme or reason. You used to have a perfect technique."

Andrew's heart returned to its normal beating. He laughed, maybe a bit too loudly. "Should I be arrested?"

"I'm calling the police right now," Beth said.

"Harsh but fair."

Beth gave Andrew a brighter smile. "Do you mind if I drive around for a little while? I always find that helps me."

"Helps with what?"

Beth pondered this for a long time. Her eyes grew distant.

"When Kurt died, I dealt with panic attacks for many years. My parents were difficult to talk to; they couldn't handle the sorrow. I just got in my car and drove and drove. On this island, there isn't far to go, so I just did circles and fell into nooks and crannies. It's like I tried to run away, but I always came back to the same place. Maybe that's the definition of insanity.

"In any case, your family is worried about you, but they trust me to know what to do. The nurse's scrubs give me some level of authority, I guess," she continued. "I told them I would have you back when you were ready to come back. No sooner than that. Is that okay with you?"

Andrew's eyes welled with tears. On the stereo, a Goo Goo Dolls song reminded him of long-ago summer nights when all he had wanted to do was just sit with Beth Leopold in a car and drive till morning.

Chapter Ten

When Beth had clocked off for the day, she hadn't envisioned Andrew Montgomery to be stationed outside of Trevor Montgomery's hospital room. There he stood: just as handsome as ever, yet more rugged and hardened, the kind of man who'd seen the dark side of the world and returned without words to explain it all. She had wanted desperately to throw her arms around him and demand that he remain on the island for good. He was her very last ounce of Kurt. He held memories of Kurt she would never know.

When the PTSD attack had begun, she had recognized it immediately. She hadn't dealt with many veterans, but the symptoms were clear as day. She had gestured to Kelli, to Steven, and said, "I think it's just a little bit too much for him right now." Her hand had found his upper back, and she'd directed him, even as he'd looked to be a million miles away. She'd led him down the hallway, down the staircase, and into the snowy parking lot to her car. With every step, his right leg had limped just a little, and she knew he'd been injured while on duty—one reason for his PTSD attack.

Now that she had him in her car with the radio on and the snow fluttering around them, she recognized the peaceful place she'd created. This was what she sometimes had to do for Will, as well; when the world's chaos turned his little head to needles, she calmed him any way she could.

Beth turned on the engine and eased them out of the parking lot. Andrew sipped more of his water and ate another Oreo, this time taking it apart like an architect studying the inner design. He slid his tongue across the icing and said, "Ah, yes. I remember this now. You're right. Eating it the other way is just not as satisfying."

How could a girl like Beth—a relative loner, beyond her few friends here and there—bridge the gap between herself and Andrew? Too much had happened. The world had shifted off its axis, and they were the scattered debris.

"How does Oak Bluffs look to you now?" she asked him softly as they eased down Circuit Avenue, past the Sacred Heart Church.

"Like a town filled with ghosts," Andrew said honestly. "But just as beautiful as ever."

"That seems to be a constant," she said with a smile.

"It's what brings the tourists in from all over the world," Andrew said with the slightest bit of sarcasm. "I can't say I blame them. I just kept a wide berth as long as I could."

Beth continued to drive without any real direction in mind. Wing Rd turned into Barnes, which snaked across the eastern side of Lagoon Pond. Andrew's face turned forever toward the window; his eyes caught everything.

In time, they crept through West Tisbury and then entered Chilmark. The landscape shifted; the heavy tourism of the previous areas fell away.

"Are you taking us to Aquinnah Cliffs?" Andrew asked suddenly.

Beth hadn't gone out to Aquinnah in a year or two. She worried about Will in every environment; she didn't need to add any cliffs to the equation.

"If you want to go there, we can go," she said.

"I do."

Aquinnah Cliffs Overlook offered glorious and sweeping views of the Atlantic Ocean, which seemed monstrous and foreboding beneath the heavy winter air. As they stood on the cliff's edge, the wind ripped into them like a kind of warning. Beth slid her hands into her coat pocket and focused on the horizon line. She didn't want to look down; it gave her the creeps.

"There it is," Andrew said softly. "I've dreamed about this view almost every month for the past seventeen years. Just when I thought I'd shaken the dreams out of my head, they came back with a vengeance. I was always glad for it, too. Like my brain wanted to give me something beautiful to look at. Something familiar. Especially while I was over there."

Beth knew he meant the Middle East.

"I think coming back was a mistake," Andrew breathed. "Claire and Charlotte call me Andy like I'm still their kid brother. Steven's kids are all grown up, and Claire and Charlotte have kids who hardly know my name. They've obviously gotten along just fine without me. I'm the forgotten Montgomery." He sucked in a breath as he looked out over the ocean below and then continued. "I keep thinking about all the family dinners they've had without me, all the Christmases and Thanksgivings and the Fourth of July parties. For the first few years, maybe they felt like there was something missing. But now? It's just been too long. I came back because Claire said Dad probably wouldn't make it. Now that he's ready to come back to the world, what? They don't need me here anymore. I would do everyone a favor if I just hopped on the ferry right now and never looked back."

Beth blinked back tears. Her eyes felt like ice against the chilly wind.

"I know it must feel that way," she whispered. "But all I can say is, I think your family has missed you much more than you know. They love you so much, Andrew."

When your parents saw me, they could hardly speak to me. I reminded them of you. I represented what could go really wrong if you didn't come back alive at all.

There was a buzzing sound. Andrew leafed into his pocket and drew out his phone.

"I don't recognize the number. I guess it's one of my siblings."

"Answer it," Beth said.

"I don't know."

Beth couldn't force him into his family. She couldn't say, *If you didn't have a family, it would be the only thing you wanted in the world.* That was inherently selfish, even if she really did believe this to be true.

When the ring cut out, another came through.

"I don't think they're going to give up on you so easily," Beth said.

But Andrew let it go to voicemail yet again. Seconds later, a message appeared on his screen, which he allowed Beth to read.

> UNKNOWN: Hey. This is Steve. Dad needs to rest, so we're headed back to the family house to have some dinner. I hope you're okay. We want to spend some time with you if you're ready. I know it's a lot at once. Let me know if there's anything I can do.

Andrew shoved his phone back into his pocket. His face

was stoic. Beth knew that she had to head off soon anyway; she had to pick up Will from his after-school therapy program. She felt anxious being in the very center of two things she very much cared about.

"Thank you for bringing me out here," Andrew said. "I can finally breathe again. Back at the hospital, I wasn't sure that would be possible."

"Don't mention it," Beth said. "You know I'd take any chance to drive Andrew Montgomery around in my car."

Andrew gave her the shadow version of his terrifically handsome teenage smile. Her heart stopped beating for a split second. He really was attractive, even in his clear anger and turmoil. She wanted to tell him how much she loved his smile, but she knew it was better not to say a word.

"Do you mind driving me back to Oak Bluffs?" he asked.

"I'm heading that way myself," she said.

Andrew's smile didn't falter as he turned back toward her car. "So. Are you ever going to tell me what your son's name is?"

Beth was surprised he had taken an interest. She had thought he would freak about it and run as far as he could in another direction.

"His name is Will. Will Leopold," she said.

"He took your name," Andrew said.

"There was no other name to take," Beth told him.

Andrew contemplated this. Obviously, there were a number of things to explain: that Will's father had been a summer fling; that she hadn't been willing to end a pregnancy, especially not after she had lost so much; that the love Will had brought into this world had blown her over with its magic.

"Will Leopold is a name suited for European kings," was all he said instead as he slipped back into her car. "He's going to be famous one day."

Chapter Eleven

Andrew had never recovered so quickly from a panic attack. Ordinarily, they were all-encompassing and left him flat on his back for the rest of the evening. Only when sleep came, if it did at all, could he find any kind of relief.

Beth brought a level of welcome calm to his frantic mind. As she drove them back toward Oak Bluffs, she crafted a conversation that lacked nostalgia and had nothing to do with today's sadness; one that brought out the life and vitality that had once brewed between them when they had been much younger kids.

Once outside the Montgomery family house, Beth heaved a sigh and said, "Every time we drive past this place, Will asks about it. He thinks it's haunted."

"The kid might be right about that," Andrew said with a wink. "Kids are always good about that, aren't they? They're always the ones who figure out what's wrong in scary movies."

"Any ghost that passes Will's path will have a lot to reckon with," Beth said. "He can be quite a handful."

"Like any other boy in the world," Andrew affirmed. "I was a monster."

Steven's truck and Claire's car had returned to the Montgomery family driveway. Their mother's car was presumably up at the hospital, and their father's was at the salvage yard somewhere, all crumpled up after the accident.

"Wish me luck," Andrew said as he popped out the side of the car. He hovered in the gap of the door and made heavy eye contact with Beth Leopold, the only woman he would have welcomed into haunting him. "It was so good to see you, Beth. Thank you for getting me out of there when I needed it."

"Don't mention it," she said. "If you stick around, maybe our paths will cross again."

Beth always had that way about her. She knew how to play "cool," and it came off so easy, as first nature as breathing. Andrew walked up the driveway and rammed his hands into his pockets. His leg continued its angry hiccup, but he hardly noticed.

When he entered the front door, the smell of New England clam chowder, his mother's glorious recipe, assaulted his nostrils. The memory of it made his mouth water on command.

"Who's that?" Claire called from the kitchen.

Charlotte appeared outside the kitchen to check. There was a splatter of chowder across her chest, and she held a glass of red wine in her hand. She grinned to show red wine-tinged teeth.

"There he is. Andy's back!"

She looked at him without anger or remorse. She looked at him playfully, with the scornful look of an older sister. This time, it didn't annoy Andrew in the least.

"Andrew! Get in here. We got the game on, and Charlotte's pouring illegally large glasses of wine," Steven called.

The kitchen jutted out to the side into a TV room, where Steven, Kelli, Abby, Gail, and another girl Andrew assumed was Rachel sat. A football game appeared on the screen. Rachel's eyes dug into him curiously just as Charlotte snuck up behind and said, "Little bro, I'm so happy you get to meet my best girl. This is Rachel."

Rachel popped up from the chair in the corner. She had a funny mix of Jason and Charlotte's features and had somehow stirred them together to craft her own unique look. Before Andrew could speak, she threw her arms around him.

"Uncle Andy! I've heard so much about you over the years."

And I only learned you existed last night.

"How is it possible that you girls are all teenagers already?" Andrew said to Gail, Abby, and Rachel as the hug broke.

"Tell me about it," Claire said as she hovered over a huge vat of clam chowder. "You blink once, Andrew, and then—whoosh. Time catches up to you."

"Come sit with us," Kelli demanded. She tapped the space beside her on the couch, one that, funnily enough, looked to be the same exact one that had existed in their family room, the room that had been dubbed 'only for family.'

Andrew did as he was told. The moment he collapsed, Charlotte appeared beside him with a glass of merlot. He clicked his glass with Kelli and with Steve before turning to click his with Gail, Rachel, and Abby's glasses of hot apple cider.

"Laura's on her way," Steven announced. "Along with Jonathon, Carrie, their babies, and Isabella."

"My three are on their way as well," Kelli said. "They were such little things when you left."

"Jonathon remembers you," Steven asserted. "We talked about it a few weeks ago, actually, around Thanksgiving time. He said he remembers playing catch with you in the backyard. Apparently, it was big news to him, the fact that his uncle was the star pitcher at the high school."

"It sounds like a story from someone else's life," Andrew said.

"You were a killer on the mound," Steven continued. "The guy at-bat never knew what was coming for him. I watched you pitch that no-hitter your junior year, remember? We went out and celebrated after, me and your buddy. What was his name?"

Kelli ribbed Steven with her elbow. That reminded Steve that he wasn't supposed to bring up Kurt's name, not that he'd remembered it.

"Oh, man. I'm so sorry about that," Steven said.

"It's okay," Andrew said. He was surprised to feel that he really meant it. "That was one of the best nights, that no-hitter. And me, you, and Kurt went out on the boat after. Laura was so mad that you got home late. Jonathon must have been just five or six."

"That's right," Steven agreed. He gave Andrew a grateful smile. "She was not thrilled."

"Who wasn't thrilled?" Laura's voice rang out from the kitchen as she entered with a platter of what looked like brownies. She grinned broadly at Andrew as she said, "Well, hey there, Andy Montgomery. Aren't you a sight for sore eyes?"

There was the sound of a screeching baby, followed by another sound of a woman doing what she could to calm that same baby. A dark voice Andrew didn't recognize said, "Let me take him."

"No, no. Go say hello to your uncle," a woman said. "I'm sure he's dying to see you again."

In actuality, Andrew was. He nearly jumped to his feet when he spotted the twenty-four-year-old version of Jonathon Montgomery: tall and broad-shouldered like all the Montgomery men, with a twinkle in his eye that reminded him of Steven as a younger man.

"Uncle Andy," he boomed. He said it like a guy who tried and failed to hide his excitement. "Man, it's good to see you."

"You're even older than I was when I left the island," Andrew said as he shook his nephew's hand.

"Don't rub it in," Jonathon said with a laugh. "Now that I have two kids of my own, I feel ancient."

"I think you still have some good years left," Andrew offered.

"I guess you probably didn't hear this, but I went on to play baseball in high school," Jonathon said.

Andrew's heart quickened. "No way."

"Yep. Pitcher on varsity all four years," Jonathon said. "I was never as good as you; they were weak years on our team."

"He's being modest." His wife, Carrie, appeared beside him with a toddler; apparently, she'd gotten the baby to go to sleep. "He was the star of the team. It's one of the reasons I fell in love with him."

Jonathon blushed heavily. "Don't listen to a single lie that comes out of her mouth. She was after my buddy on third base, but he was already taken."

Carrie rolled her eyes and swatted Jonathon across the arm. Charlotte walked forward, passed them both glasses of wine, and told everyone that the clam chowder was almost ready. The screen door slammed closed again to bring Isabella, who was the spitting image of Laura around the time Andrew had met her for the first time. Behind her was Christine Sheridan, the same woman Andrew had seen on Charlotte's doorstep. In her hands, she held several French-style baguettes.

"Christine! What are you doing here?" Charlotte asked brightly.

"I heard you guys were having a little dinner get-together, and I wanted to make sure you had enough bread," she said. "Freshly baked by yours truly."

"Christine, you're too generous," Claire said as she accepted the baguettes in her arms. "Seriously, this will go perfectly with..."

"Clam chowder?" Christine finished. "How could you have anything else? Especially with Andy back after so long." She gave Andrew a tiny wave and added, "I bet you hardly remember me. I left when you were just a kid."

Andrew shrugged. "Guess we're both back now. How ya been?"

Charlotte ushered Christine in and threw an arm around her. "She's been all over the world, is how she's been. What was it you were telling me? Paris? Stockholm? London?"

"Yada yada yada," Christine said. "But now I'm back where I belong. I do the desserts and pastries at the Sunrise Cove Bistro. My boyfriend is the chef."

"Wow. Full circle," Andrew said.

Christine blushed. "It's been a pretty big year for me and my sisters. I never imagined any of us would return to the Vineyard. Now, I can't imagine my life without it."

Kelli's children arrived after that: Sam, Josh, and Lexi. Andrew could hardly believe that this full-grown teenager, Lexi, had been the teensy babe he'd held in his eighteen-year-old arms. Apparently, they had all heard tons of stories about him; they spoke to him as though he was a celebrity.

Claire ushered everyone to the big dining room for clam chowder, freshly-baked bread, heaps of salad, homemade cheese from the nearby dairy farm, and buckets of wine. Christine bid everyone goodbye; she had to return to Zach for the night. When she left the house and disappeared, Claire mentioned, "She used to be so upset when we were growing up. Who could blame her, though, after Aunt Anna died and with Susan leaving the island right afterward."

"She looks very happy," Andrew said.

"She really does," Charlotte affirmed as she decorated the edges of her plate with salad and cherry tomatoes. "There has been a bit of drama in the Sheridan house lately. Lola's only daughter, Audrey, is pregnant and Christine has offered to raise the baby for the first few years so Audrey can go back to college. What else? Oh, Amanda, Susan's daughter, is about to get married. And they also discovered Aunt Anna was having an affair with Stan Ellis, and he was with her when the accident happened."

"That's a whole lot of something," Andrew said with a hearty laugh. "I thought I had problems."

"We all have problems," Steven said as he broke off a healthy dose of baguette. "The Sheridan sisters have always handled their problems with style."

Aunt Anna's funeral was one of Andrew's first really powerful memories. He'd been eight years old at the time, and his mother had forced him to wear a suit, one that made his neck itch terribly throughout the service. The Sheridan sisters had been inconsolable throughout, Lola especially, as she had been the youngest, the one more apt to fall apart. There had been a great deal of bickering after the service. Andrew's mother had struggled with Wes. There had been a number of discussions between his mother and father about "how to help Wes" and, "what should we do about the girls?" As an eight-year-old, Andrew had only known one thing: what had happened couldn't be taken back. Nothing would ever be the same again.

The clam chowder was sinfully delicious. It tasted every bit the same as their mother's and perhaps the tiniest bit better, although Andrew would have never informed Kerry Montgomery of this opinion unless he was after a beating. He dunked Christine's perfect baguette into the sludge-like goodness and closed his eyes as he chewed. Since his departure from the island, he'd eaten perhaps thousands of TV dinners, fast food take-out, and random bags of chips. He had forced himself to forget what it meant to eat something made with love.

"Was a real shocker to see Beth Leopold today," Steven said as they finished up the meal. "I guess I forgot about her over the years."

"She has a young son," Charlotte said. "Will. Poor thing has autism."

Andrew's heart sank. Beth hadn't informed him of this. It added color to the sadness behind her eyes, the truth of the weight of her life.

"It was such a horrible thing when her parents passed," Claire said. "I thought Beth was going to break in half."

"She might have if it wasn't for Will," Charlotte said. "She had to be strong for him."

"Where did she take you today?" Steven asked Andrew. "You guys were gone quite a while."

"We just went for a drive," Andrew said. "It calmed me down a lot."

Steven studied Andrew's face contemplatively. He looked on the verge of asking a question that had way too much in its answer: *what the heck happened to you over there?*

But Claire interjected before Steven had the chance. "Who wants to help clean up?"

"I will," Andrew said immediately. "I owe it to you. That was one of the best meals I've had in my life, or at least, in the past seventeen years."

"Let's not make our baby brother clean up," Charlotte said. "He's been gone all these years. We shouldn't put him to work."

"I insist," Andrew said. This would allow him to avoid any uncomfortable conversations that could pop up.

Once at the sink, his leg tried its best to seize upon him. Andrew placed his elbow on the counter to support himself as he sipped his wine. Claire arrived with the first stack of bowls and winked at him. "Thanks for doing this."

Kelli appeared with another stack as Andrew ran the water. Steam billowed around them as she beamed at him. "What if you wash and I dry?"

"A bit of teamwork in the Montgomery clan?" Andrew heard himself ask.

"That kind of thing. Yep," Kelli said. "If you think you can handle it?"

"I've been a lone wolf all these years." He chuckled.

"Oh, you mean, like this?" Kelli suddenly dropped her head back and wolf-howled toward the ceiling.

The sound and the look of it made Andrew burst into outrageous laughter. Carrie rushed into the kitchen and hissed, "You guys! I don't want to wake the baby." She looked on the verge of attacking them.

When Carrie disappeared again, Kelli winced and said, "She almost tore us to pieces."

"And she would have been in the right," Andrew said.

"Sure. I remember what that was like. If anyone messes with your baby's sleep schedule, it's grounds for murder."

Andrew scrubbed the bowls and plates and passed them over to Kelli. Between bowls, Kelli snapped on the radio and hummed along. After a few rounds of forks and spoons, Andrew said, "You know, I was reading about Charlotte's wedding thing in a magazine when Claire called."

Kelli's eyebrows snapped up. "That's eerie, isn't it?" After a pause, she added, "But not as eerie as you actively purchasing a wedding magazine."

Andrew chuckled. "Are you suggesting my heart is too black to read about the joys of marriage?"

"Naw. I saw the way you looked at Beth Leopold today. I know your heart is still the color of cotton candy," Kelli teased.

Andrew rolled his eyes. "Yeah. Right." He leaned toward her then and whispered. "What happened with Jason? Obviously, Charlotte was out west with some guy called Everett, but I can't get a full read on what's up."

Kelli's eyes grew shadowed. "He died in a fishing accident. It was awful. To be honest with you, Charlotte has only just begun to act like herself again. Claire and I thought she would never find a way out of that black hole. But that's the thing about life, isn't it? The only way through is... through."

Andrew's throat felt tight. How dare he think, after all these years, that he was the only one of his siblings who had gone through trauma and horror? He scrubbed at another bowl and said, "I should have been here." The words were a surprise to him.

"It's okay that you weren't," Kelli breathed. "Charlotte understands. We all do. At least as much as we can. I know we've missed so much. It seemed like you were always on one tour or another when we tried to get in touch with you."

"I was pretty purposeful with that, I guess. I didn't want it to be easy to find me," Andrew admitted.

"Oh, really?" Kelli said with a sarcastic smile. "Huge shocker."

Andrew blushed as he sipped a bit more wine. "You never lost that sense of humor after all these years? I would have thought you would have turned into an upstanding lady by now."

Kelli scoffed. "A lady? I can't believe you would insult me like that."

Chapter Twelve

Lexi, Gail, Abby, and Rachel ambled into the kitchen a few minutes later. At seventeen, fifteen, and fourteen, they were among the most terrifying creatures Andrew had witnessed as of late. They looked at the world with an understanding he would never know. They were on the verge of their entire lives.

"Hey girls," Kelli said. "You come in here to help me and your Uncle Andy?"

"What? No way," Lexi said with a funny smile. "We're here because the speaker system is taken over with the game, and we want to practice our dance."

"Oh, no. Here we go again," Kelli said playfully as she leaned back against the counter. "The same routine or a different one?"

"Mom, come on. The dances change constantly," Lexi said. "And if we're going to go viral, we have to keep working."

Lexi spoke with the matter-of-fact tone that Kelli had once worn with her younger sisters and brother. She placed her phone on the counter and connected it to a Bluetooth speaker further up the counter. It bubbled up then offered a firm, "You are now connected to MONTGOMERY BLUETOOTH."

"Easy as that," Kelli said.

Lexi, Rachel, Gail, and Abby got into a line after that. They crossed their arms over their chests and nodded their heads in time to the beat four times in a row. Then, their right foot burst out to the side in almost perfect unison, and they built up the first several steps in what seemed to be an elaborate routine over the top of a horrible pop song.

At least, the song was horrible in Andrew's ears.

When they stumbled on a dance move, Lexi stopped the music and instructed the other girls on where they had gone wrong. Andrew watched, perplexed. Kelli's elbow found his rib as she said, "I bet this is like watching aliens from another planet for you, isn't it?"

"Something like that."

Lexi turned and arched her eyebrow with curiosity. "Do you not know this song, Uncle Andy?"

"Never heard it in my life," Andrew told her.

The girls exchanged gasps. Even Kelli chuckled and said, "Wow. I feel like that song's been crammed into my skull. I'll never lose it."

"Yeah. It played on every single radio station all summer long," Rachel informed him. "Where were you?"

Mostly alone in my apartment, trying to relearn how to walk.

"Guess I missed out," Andrew said.

"Were you living under a rock?" Gail asked.

"I guess I was. And it wasn't even a very nice rock," Andrew said with a smile.

The girls giggled. He could see it reflected back in their eyes: they thought their Uncle Andy was rather funny. This was all he could have ever dreamed for.

"All right. Let's get him in the group," Abby said suddenly.

The other girls looked perplexed. Andrew muttered to Kelli under his breath, "Are they talking about me like I'm not here?"

"I think they're having a business meeting," Kelli whispered back. "You know how it is in the entertainment industry. It's hard to get everyone on board."

The girls completed their meeting, turned to face him, and cleared their throats in unison. If their goal was to operate as a kind of in-unison-forever dance-troupe, Andrew thought they had a pretty good chance.

"We've decided to offer you a place in our dance troupe," Lexi announced. She seemed to be their leader, as she was the oldest.

"I see," Andrew said.

"The thing is, there's a higher likelihood of going viral if you include an older family member in your dance video," she continued. "Like, people always go viral with their dads, for example."

"And we've asked our dads. They don't want anything to do with it," Gail affirmed.

"I see," Andrew said. "So, your last chance has fallen on my shoulders, huh?"

"Don't think of it that way," Lexi told him. "Think of it as an opportunity to let the world see you shine."

Andrew had never been a gullible person. In the previous seventeen-some years, in fact, he had grown increasingly pessimistic, prone to not believing what he read in the news or what people told him.

But now, with these four bright-faced and optimistic teenage girls in front of him, he was frozen. How could he possibly tell them how little he thought of the internet? How could he explain that he hadn't moved his body in a dancing motion in years?

"Okay. I'll give it a try," he told them.

Kelli's jaw dropped. Her eyes glittered with good humor. "Wow. Uncle Andy. You're really back, aren't you?"

"Don't rub it in," he said as he took a delicate limp toward the girls. As he went, he smacked his hand on his thigh and said, "Just so you girls know, I have a bum right leg. I can still put weight on it; I can still move it. I just might have to switch up a few moves."

"No problem," Lexi told him. "When I twisted my ankle in cheerleading, I learned to switch up some of the moves so I could still perform."

That was the funny thing about kids. They didn't allow the world to weigh them down. They found ways to ease around the pain and move forward. It was something humans necessarily forgot along the way.

Why was that?

The girls instructed him as best as they could, given the circumstances. They showed him the head nods and the hip-tilts and the foot motions, which they eventually sped up to match the sound of the song. They played the same song so many times that it, too, was crammed into the back of Andrew's skull. After a while, he even found that he rather liked it.

Thirty minutes later, they managed to record their first dance. Kelli held the phone as they performed in the space near the piano in the living area, and her face was stoic and firm the entire time to ensure that she didn't shake the phone around. When they finished, the girls and Andrew hovered around the phone to watch. Although there were a few hiccups, a few forgotten motions, Andrew had done better than all right. The girls made sure to tell him how pleased they were.

"If this goes viral, we might need to have you back in the troupe," Lexi told him. "I hope you're ready for that."

Before filming, Kelli had snuck a tray of chocolate chip cookies into the oven. On cue, the oven timer blared out, and she shuffled back into the kitchen to draw out the gooey batch.

Andrew re-entered the kitchen to fully take in the sight: his favorite sister, a tray of freshly-baked cookies, and Christmas decorations hanging in every corner. It was enough to take his breath away.

Gail snuck up behind him and switched the song on the Bluetooth to an old Christmas classic: "I'll Be Home for Christmas."

"That's a little on the nose, don't you think?" Andrew said with a laugh.

Gail shrugged. "It's a beautiful song. It always makes my mom cry."

Claire entered the kitchen and placed her hands on her hips. "What always makes Mom cry?"

"This song," Gail said. She stretched out her arms and beckoned for her mother to come toward her. Claire did. She scooped her daughter up in a hug and then pretended to ball-room dance with her to the gorgeous, sweeping music.

Lexi and Rachel joined up into a partnership; then, Laura and Steven even joined, with Steve insisting that he'd only come into the kitchen to steal a chocolate chip cookie. Kelli tapped Andrew's elbow and said, "I don't want to beg, but..." and Andrew flung his arm around her, grabbed her hand, and twirled her round-and-round, the way she had done for him when he'd been just a little boy and eager to spin around until he got dizzy.

These moments were blissful. They ached with nostalgia yet cried out with something else: the urgent desire to make something new with the people Andrew loved the most in the world. Maybe it was the drama of the Christmas music; maybe it was the string instruments getting to him or the bravado of the singer's voice. It didn't matter, though. Regardless of it all, he was home.

A shadow appeared in the doorway. For a long moment, Andrew forced himself to avoid it, like a memory he didn't want to look at too closely. But as the song closed out, the shadow stepped forward. Lexi dropped her arms from around Rachel; Gail and Claire moved to the side. Instantly, Kelli's smile dropped, and she drew her hands away from Andrew so she could greet the newcomer to the room.

Mike.

The man was now middle-aged. It was strange to see him: the same anger permeated through the back of his eyes, but his skin had brewed up a healthy round of wrinkles, and his cheeks sagged just the slightest bit. He was still strong and muscular but not exactly the kind of guy Andrew had punched all those years ago. He wore a beautiful suit that told the world just how important he was.

"Hey babe," Kelli said.

Another Christmas song began on the Bluetooth. Mike looked at the Bluetooth speaker like he wanted to order it to be burned.

"What's all this?" he asked.

"Just a dance party," Lexi said. She had lost all the spark she'd had previously; she looked at her father like he had more power than he deserved.

"Is there any chowder left?" Mike asked.

"Of course," Kelli replied. She snapped into action. In seconds, some of the delicious soup was in a bowl, turning round and round in the microwave.

As the microwave roared, Steve, Laura, Gail, Rachel, and Lexi abandoned the kitchen. Andrew couldn't find an escape, and Michael blocked his way. Claire remained, tilting her weight from side to side like she wanted to say something but didn't have the strength.

"Hey Mike," Andrew said. He was surprised that he was the first to say anything.

When Mike lifted his eyes to Andrew's, he felt it: the

memory of the last time they'd seen one another. Mike still hated him for it. The anger remained in the air between them.

"Hey Andy," he said flatly.

"The girls taught their Uncle Andy one of their famous dances," Kelli said. Her voice was as bright as it could be, and it sounded terribly false in Andrew's ears. "They think he's their secret to going viral."

Mike didn't bother to answer. The microwave beeped, and Kelli stirred up the chowder before she passed it over to her husband. He didn't thank her before he stalked out of the room to eat in front of the game.

Anxiously, Kelli grabbed a cookie from the tray and nibbled at the edge. She then wandered out of the room after him, leaving a Kelli-sized hole in Andrew's heart all over again.

Andrew's eyes found Claire's immediately. She shook her head delicately as she stepped toward him. With a cookie in her hand, she whispered, "I really haven't seen much of Kelli lately."

"What do you mean?"

"She keeps her distance these days," Claire said. "Mike's pissed almost everyone off in the family, and I think it embarrasses her that she's stuck around this long. I've only talked to her about it a handful of times. Each time, she deflected as best as she could. You know how we in the Montgomery family are Olympic deflectors."

"Ain't that the truth," Andrew said with a heavy sigh. "I just would have thought, after all this time, she would have found a way out."

"Time is a strange thing," Claire said. "I have to think it went like this. She was in her late twenties. She had three very young children. After a fight between her little brother and her husband, her little brother took off and went to war. The whole thing devastated her, and she blames herself for it. I think she wanted to prove to herself that she had done the right thing, but the guilt has destroyed her."

Andrew shook his head as devastation clouded his vision. "I never wanted her to live like that. It's not her fault I left."

"She never wanted you to live the way you did, either. But now, we're here together. Maybe we can pick up the pieces as we go," Claire returned.

Chapter Thirteen

L ater that week, Beth received word that Trevor Montgomery would begin physical therapy with her over the next few days. She hovered over the pot of macaroni and cheese she had cooked up for Will as her heart pounded. This physical therapy was the sort of task she had done countless times. The joy that came with giving someone their freedom back after an accident was the kind of joy that gave you wings. In this case, however, the stakes felt terribly high. She couldn't make any kind of mistake. It was for Andrew. It was for Kerry. It was for Steve and Kelli and Charlotte and Claire. But most of all, it was for their shared past, the sights and sounds they had all experienced together, and the fact that once upon a time, they'd all known Kurt when he was alive.

The morning of Trevor's first physical therapy session started out like any other. Little Will scrambled into the kitchen with his shirt on both inside-out and backward. After he fixed it himself, he sat for a plate of eggs, turkey bacon, and toast, which Beth tried to cook up for him every morning, as she knew it helped his anxiety ten-fold if he had something good in his belly. Then, they gathered up his homework assignments, his books, and the one toy he was allowed to bring to school before they stuffed themselves in their coats and rushed off into the chilly morning.

As there was a bit of extra time, Beth decided to park in the lot near the school and walk her son to the front door. He didn't require it, not at eight, but she always took pleasure in it: the sounds of their feet crunching through the snow and the chill of the air against her cheeks. He told her wonderful things about a new dinosaur he liked, and she listened intently. She needed to remember it for next time, whether that next time be tomorrow or three years from now.

When they were no more than fifteen yards from the front door of the school, a snowball smacked across Will's stomach. The whack was a hard one, the kind that left a red mark. Beth's eyes found the perpetrator immediately: a kid in one of the other classes who sometimes liked to tease Will because of his autism.

Panic overwhelmed Beth, although she knew better than to show it. Will's face crumpled up as Beth fell to her knees to whisper to him. "It's okay! He's playing with you," she tried. All the while, the young boy's laughter rang out like a horrible chorus.

"No, he's not," Will wailed.

"Baby, it's okay." She held him tightly against her and placed her chin on his shoulder as he shook. She held him like that until the kid got bored and paraded into the school with his other friends. She held him like that long after the line of parent-drop-off had receded and minutes after the first bell had sounded. It became clear that Will wouldn't enter the school that day; she had to make alternate plans.

Unfortunately, when she called her usual babysitter, she found that the poor girl had a horrible case of bronchitis. Her backup babysitter was off the island looking at colleges. This left Beth in a pickle. So, she decided to bring Will with her to the hospital. It wasn't the first time she'd had to do it.

Beth and Will Leopold entered the breakroom down the hall from the physical therapy room. They unzipped their coats, removed their hats, and stuffed all their belongings in Beth's little locker. Ellen entered as they performed this routine, placed her hand on her waist, and said, "Well, look who we have here? Is that William Leopold?"

Will turned and delivered an adorable grin to Ellen, one of his favorite people in the world. "Hello, Ellen," he said. "Good morning to you."

"And a good morning to you, sir," Ellen replied.

Ellen gave Beth a curious glance, to which Beth just shrugged. Obviously, he'd struggled with school that morning. Obviously, they'd had to make other arrangements. As a mother of an autistic child, she'd had to learn how to innovate.

"What's your schedule today, Beth?" Ellen asked.

"I have Trevor Montgomery in an hour or so," Beth returned.

Ellen's eyes turned toward Will. "I don't think many nurses will be in the breakroom today. You might have to set old William up in the little room alongside the therapy room. The one with the glass walls."

"Not a problem," Beth said, even as her heart jumped into her throat. "We brought your iPad, didn't we, bud? And you can just sit and play your games and read your book."

Beth had invested in a series of educational games for just these moments when she couldn't get Will to go to school, but she still wanted to broaden his mind. Will was a smart kid, perhaps too smart, and he took to language and words and mathematics with zeal. It was just people he had trouble with.

An hour later, Beth set Will up in the little side room alongside the physical therapy room. As the nurse wheeled in Trevor

Montgomery, Will crossed his legs beneath him in the chair and brought up his favorite spelling game on his iPad. He shooed his mother out of the room as he said, "I have to practice spelling now, Mommy. I'll let you know if I need anything."

"Okay, baby," Beth said softly as she turned back toward the bigger room. Slowly, she clipped the door closed behind her, grateful that he seemed much calmer now than he had been.

Beth greeted Trevor's nurse and took the clipboard from her, which revealed an analysis of the drugs he'd been on, and what had happened thus far, that sort of thing. Although he had broken his arm, his legs were just tight, battered, and bruised, and he needed assistance finding strength again. There was the possibility that he wouldn't walk properly for a few months or more.

"Hey there, Mr. Montgomery," Beth said, her voice as friendly and open as she could make it. "I heard a rumor around here that you took quite a tumble."

"That's one way to put it," Mr. Montgomery said. His smile was infectious. One of his large hands tapped at the bandage still wrapped around his head. "I'm just glad I still got the old thinker going. Sharp as a knife."

"They can't take you down that easily," Beth said.

"That's right."

Beth started Trevor out as easily as she could. They performed stretches together and talked about his limitations and where he should push himself over the next few days. "You have to learn how to recognize the difference between strain and pain," Beth told him. "A tiny bit of strain is okay; if the pain becomes like flashes of light, then you know you're taking it too far."

Trevor nodded, then asked appropriate questions, and remained genuine and focused until his time came to an end. Throughout the session, Beth managed, somehow, to forget

Andrew Montgomery and remained wholly in her role as a rehabilitation nurse.

It was only when Trevor turned his eyes toward the adjoining room, spotted Will on his iPad, and asked, "What is that young boy doing here?" that Beth began to crumble with emotion.

"He's my son," she said. Her voice sounded choked up. "He had a little bit of a problem this morning. The real world seemed a little too mean. He wasn't so sure he wanted to go to school today, so he's doing his own learning here. He's terribly good at teaching himself."

"We all could take a page out of his book," Trevor affirmed. "I think one of the most important things in this life is being able to teach yourself."

Beth's smile grew wider. "He asks some of the wildest and most introspective questions I've heard in my life. I think he's about fifty times smarter than I am. There are just some things he can't handle."

Trevor nodded contemplatively. It was clear he had a great deal on his mind. His free hand hovered over the wheel of his wheelchair as he said, "I think my own son, Andy, had some trouble with the real world, too. I didn't know how to help him."

Beth stopped breathing altogether. Trevor's eyes remained toward the ground, as though if he looked at Beth as he told her, the words would be too heavy.

"Kerry told me he's in town," Trevor continued. "I scared him away seventeen years ago, if you can believe it. That's about half his life that I've missed, just because I had all these opinions about the way he was supposed to be, the way he needed to live his life. I'm so surprised he's in town. Heck, I wouldn't be surprised if he already ran off the island. Why would he want to mess around with an old man like me? I have nothing to offer him."

Beth remained frozen. She knew she had to say something —something to help repair this father-son relationship, one that had started off a mess and remained one until Andrew had abandoned it altogether.

"The point is, you're doing a good job with your son. You recognize his needs. You seem to know how to help him become the kind of man he's meant to be," Trevor continued. "On my end of things, I think it might be too late."

Beth's voice crackled. "I don't think it's too late."

Trevor gave a sad shrug. "It depends, doesn't it? Right now, I'm stuck in the hospital for a few more days. I have no way of knowing what's up in that kid's mind. He always seemed to hate me. I always felt that when he looked at me, he saw a monster."

Chapter Fourteen

Andrew's phone reflected back the date and time: December 15. 7:46 in the morning. He rubbed his eyes with chapped hands and blinked at the gray light that hovered over him. He had slept in his childhood bedroom, just as he'd done the night before that, and the feel of it, the familiarity of it, still shocked him. He had a funny instinct to put on a Blink-182 song, run his fingers through his hair, and head off to high school. He could still hear it: the screech of his locker, the yelp of the girls as they gossiped their way to class, the intercom announcements: *Today's lunch is hotdogs, hamburgers, and French fries. Yippee.*

But no. He was thirty-five years old. He could feel it in his bones, in the strange jump of his right leg, and in the haze of his head. He placed his feet on the ground beside the bed and rubbed his temples. Time to get up and, what? Spend another day in the shadows of his family house? Try and fail yet again to force himself up to the hospital to speak to his father? His mother had come home only a handful of times, each time to grab a shower or a change of clothes or a book his father had requested. "He can't even focus on the words, but he keeps planning on trying again," she'd informed him.

Andrew padded downstairs. He expected to find a creaking, empty house, but when he appeared in the kitchen, he found Kelli seated at the table, her shoulders hunched and her face pale and morose. There was a cup of coffee in front of her. It no longer looked warm or even appetizing.

"Kelli," Andrew said. "Hey."

Kelli grimaced. "Hey."

Andrew wasn't sure what to say. Had she slept at the house that night? Had something happened between her and Mike? Was this a common occurrence?

Andrew brewed another pot of coffee. Wordlessly, he poured out Kelli's cold cup and refilled it with a warm brew. He also added just a touch of milk before he placed it in front of her again. She shook her head slightly and said, "Thank you. You didn't have to do that. I totally spaced for a second."

"Don't worry about it," he told her as he returned to sit beside her. He sipped his own cup of coffee and watched as her face changed. Her eyes began to lighten.

"I have something for you. For us," she said as she jumped to her feet. She reached into the cabinet and drew out a box of Lucky Charms, their old favorite snack. With a flourish, she poured them both heaping bowls and then added just the right amount of milk.

"I see you haven't forgotten the perfect Lucky Charms recipe," he told her with a sly grin.

"You think I could forget that? We had that down to a science," she told him.

They lifted their bowls and clinked them together. "Cheers," they said in unison, which made them fall into fits of laughter.

"I remember when I introduced you to this stuff," Kelli said as she chewed on the sugary-tart mallows. "I used to sneak them in so that Mom couldn't see. We'd eat and watch cartoons and call it our secret."

"I remember," Andrew said. "Maybe that's where I first started to go wrong. My love for Lucky Charms pushed me down a dark road."

Kelli laughed. "I don't know about that. If you look at any of our lives too closely, it's clear that none of us have any of this figured out."

As the marshmallows disintegrated in the milk, Andrew placed his spoon to the side, folded his hands, and said, "Kelli, you know you can talk to me about anything, right? I'm not a teenager anymore."

Kelli bit hard on her lower lip, so hard that a small droplet of blood oozed down. She hurriedly wiped at it with part of her napkin.

"I know that," she breathed. "Honestly, I planned to sneak out of here before you woke up."

"You thought you could leave me to eat Lucky Charms alone?" Andrew asked with a laugh.

"I guess that would have been unfair," Kelli said. "It's just me and Mike keep getting into it. He's gotten somehow crueler since Josh and Sam moved out. Lexi's normally busy with friends, and Mike only has me there to rip into. He doesn't treat me like a human any longer. Maybe he never did." She paused and took a small sip of her coffee.

"In any case, I've tried to hide it from Steve, Claire, and Charlotte as best as I can. Mom doesn't know I stayed the night last night. That's maybe the worst part of all of this. I always wanted to be like Mom and Dad. In sickness and in health, as they're showing us now—through everything. I wanted my marriage to be together until the end. I just don't know how to move forward with him. Especially now that you're back and all these memories are..."

She trailed off as she rubbed her temples. "I'm sorry. I don't want to bring up all the bad blood between us. It's poisonous to look at it too long."

"No. It stands to reason that my return would affect all of you. It's selfish of me to think about how hard it is on me and me alone," Andrew said.

Kelli sighed. "There you go again."

"What?"

"You always seem to see everything so clearly," she said. "I always thought that was why you had to leave the Vineyard. You couldn't lie to yourself anymore. You wanted to know what else was out there.

"Yeah, this island can be filled with lies sometimes. Aunt Anna cheating on Wes all those years ago? And then her death on the boat with her lover? That was hidden for years, and we had no idea. It's like, on the Vineyard, we're ready to pretend to be something we're not. Me, the perfect wife, mother, sister, and daughter. In actuality, I was hardly the perfect mother, and I have a loveless and verbally abusive marriage."

Andrew's heart darkened. He lifted his spoon again and stirred the last remains of his cereal.

"What I mean is, the family is messy. Welcome back to the mess," Kelli said with a sad laugh.

Andrew dropped his chin to his chest. How could he possibly explain to her just how alone he'd been over the years? How could he explain that all he wanted was the family mess since it was the exact opposite of the emptiness he had lived through for so long?

"I don't know what's going to happen next," Andrew said. "All I can really say, Kel, is that I'm happy to be here with you."

Andrew reached across the table and held onto her hand. A single tear drew a line from her eye to her chin.

"And I'm so glad to be here with you, too," she whispered.

* * *

Kelli made the decision to stick around at the old family estate, as she called it, for the rest of the day. "Mike's always in and out during the day, meeting clients and friends and co-workers. I don't want to get in his way. The minute one of his real estate deals goes south, he turns into a kind of monster."

Andrew suggested they pile into the family room and watch old movies. Kelli poured herself a second helping of Lucky Charms.

"Yeah, me too," Andrew said. Kelli tossed the box to him so he could top himself off.

"Time to have a trash day with my best bud!" she cried.

In the family room, they browsed through their mother and father's DVD and VHS collection and made a pile of "must watch" and "maybe watch."

"The day is still young," Andrew said. "We have time for at least five or six."

"We'd better throw a Christmas movie or two in there, for good measure," Kelli said.

The Christmas film they chose was, naturally, *Home Alone,* while the others were: *Back to the Future, The Mummy, The Mummy Returns* (which, in their opinion, was one of the worst films ever made), *Jurassic Park,* and *Sleepless in Seattle,* which they were both complete suckers for.

"I remember you used to watch this and cry," Kelli teased.

"Come on! Meg Ryan and Tom Hanks, out there looking for love? Who could resist?"

And then their movie marathon began. Throughout the first film and even the second, Andrew kept glancing toward his sister, just to make sure she was actually there. How could this even be real? How could he be there with her after all this time?

Luckily, the heaviness of those feelings still allowed him plenty of time to laugh at the ridiculousness of the movies they watched, gasp playfully as one of the dinosaurs attacked another scientist, and especially as Samuel L. Jackson said, "Hold onto your butts," which he now remembered he and Kelli quoting like crazy back when the movie had first come out in the nineties.

Around three-thirty in the afternoon, *Sleepless in Seattle* cut out halfway through the film. Apparently, the DVD was scratched. Kelli got up to stretch her legs and attempt to clean the back. At that moment, the screen door screeched open and slammed shut to reveal their mother.

Kerry Montgomery beamed at them. She looked as though she'd lost ten years off her age. She stretched her hands out toward them and said, "Your father is cleared to come home in just a few days!"

"That's wonderful news, Mom."

But there wasn't much time to celebrate. After the hugging and the extra round of questions to figure out their father's status, Kelli and Andrew were ordered to work.

"This place is hardly ready for Christmas," Kerry told them as she snapped her hands on her waist and gave the family room a once-over.

"There's some holly and stuff in the kitchen," Andrew said.

"Andrew, I know you've been gone a long time, but do you really expect me to stop at just-holly-in-the-kitchen during a year like this?" his mother demanded.

A list was drawn up: the kind of list that would have made even the editor of *Home and Gardens* envious. At least three Christmas trees had to be purchased, apparently; a large list of ingredients had to be bought to account for the number of Christmas cookies that needed to be baked; plus, there were meals to plan, now that their father would be home. Naturally, it fell to Andrew to put up the Christmas lights around the house, as Trevor couldn't manage it this year.

At this, his mother's eyes traced down toward his leg. He

could feel her begin to ask him something like, *Are you sure you can really do that?*

"I got it, Mom," he said. "Just tell me where the lights are."

"They're in the garage with the rest of the decorations," his mother breathed. "I can't believe it. It's December 15, and this house has hardly a lick of Christmas to show for it. Let's set to work."

The plight of Tom Hanks and Meg Ryan soon flew out of Andrew and Kelli's minds to make room for the reckless nature of the next hours. As it was the end of the school day and very nearly the end of the semester, it was decided that Lexi come along with them on their errands. Kelli drove a van with Kerry in the passenger and Andrew in the second row. Lexi hopped in after pick-up and beamed at Andrew. "Hey, Uncle Andy," she said. "Did Grandma kidnap you for the Christmas decorating extravaganza?"

"You should count yourself lucky that I think you're artistic enough for the task, Miss Lexi," Kerry said from the front.

Lexi cackled as she shrugged off her backpack and settled in beside Andrew. It was decided that they would head to the Christmas tree farm first; this way, they could get out there, grab three trees, pile them atop Kelli's car, and head back before nightfall. Once at the Christmas tree farm, Kerry's eyes dug into Andrew until he popped forward, grabbed the chainsaw himself, and then headed for the lines and lines of glittering, snow-capped trees.

Lexi helped Andrew pick out the three best: one bigger one for the front living room, a cozier, fat one for the family room, and another for the sunroom, where usually, the women gathered over Christmastime to read magazines and warm themselves in the sunlight like lizards.

"I don't know if you know this, Lexi, but most families in the United States don't need more than one Christmas tree,"

Andrew said as he revved the chainsaw for the second time, poised to attack that fat family room tree.

Lexi giggled. "I'm surprised she didn't demand six or seven and another ten to give to Grandpa's doctors."

"She has a way with that, doesn't she?"

"She likes to take care of people," Lexi affirmed. "She's tried her darndest with her brother, Great Uncle Wes. She was at the Sheridan house almost every day the past few months, checking up on him and taking him to appointments and stuff. I know Mom's worried."

Everyone in this family seems worried about everyone else, like a merry-go-round of worries.

Andrew limped each tree back to the car, grateful that his leg felt strong, even in its slowness. He and Kelli piled the trees atop the van, then strapped them down with a spare piece of rope Kelli had in the back. "It's from waterskiing last summer," Kelli said with a laugh. "Around Christmas time, summer always feels like a million years ago."

Back at the house, Kerry Montgomery had orders and plenty of them. "Kelli, you head back to the grocery store to stock up on baking supplies. Andrew, I need you to arrange all of the trees in their tree stands. Make sure to water them enough. And you, Lexi, do you think you could bring out all the Christmas decorations from the attic? Andrew, when you finish up the trees, you can head out and line the house with lights. Just make sure you keep yourself stable up there."

Lexi and Andrew exchanged heavy glances, ones that simmered with both annoyance and overwhelming joy. Andrew lifted a hand and Lexi high-fived it.

"Let's get to work, team," Andrew said to her.

"Uncle Andy and Lexi on the hunt for Christmas cheer," she returned with a funny smile.

Andrew nearly froze atop that ladder later. His knees clacked together as he tacked the string of lights across the top of the house, furrowing his brow as he went. He couldn't help but visualize himself as Chevy Chase in *Christmas Vacation*: shocking himself wildly with the lights and falling to his backside below. It was a funny image on-screen, but nothing he wanted to recreate just then.

It took a little over an hour. By the time he hobbled back down from the ladder and returned to the family room, a few newcomers had joined the movie-watching-extravaganza. Steve and his daughter, Isabella, grinned with big cups of hot cocoa in their hands; Kelli and Lexi hovered around the Christmas tree and added bulbs to it as *How the Grinch Stole Christmas* played on-screen. His mother crossed her hands over her lap and turned her eyes up toward him. Her smile told him that all the work he'd done out there was worth it. She was thrilled.

"Can I get you some hot cocoa, Andy?" she asked as she hopped up. "Maybe with a little bit of rum in it?"

"Sounds good, Mom." Andrew limped into the kitchen after his mother and watched as she boiled the water and rubbed her palms over the bubbles.

"Thank you for doing that, Andy. You did good," his mother said. "I can see the reflection of the lights across the snow. Your father will be so thrilled that you got them up for him. He dreads it more and more every year. Now that he's over seventy, well... things get harder."

His mother turned absently to grab the cocoa container. As she reached, Andrew stepped up behind her and wrapped his arms around her. She turned into the hug as Andrew's shoulders shook. He'd felt it like a crashing wave: he loved his mother terribly and he had missed her with every fiber of his being.

"What was that for?" his mother asked as their hug parted. Her eyes glittered with tears.

"I've missed you so much. I'm just so happy to be home," he told her.

"We've missed you so much, too. We love you more than

life itself," she said as she pressed a kiss to his cheek. "It's so wonderful to have you home for the holidays."

* * *

Hours later, Steve, Isabella, Kelli, and Lexi were all bundled up to head home. Andrew made heavy eye contact with Kelli, squeezed her wrist, and whispered, "You'll tell me if you need anything, right?"

"It's time to head home," Kelli said under her breath.

In the hollowness of the aftermath, Kerry and Andrew sat alone in the family room with another round of hot cocoa and just enough rum to keep their minds at peace. They were in the middle of another Christmas classic from the 'oos—*The Holiday*. Andrew had been in Afghanistan when they'd screened it for them. He remembered it: the strange heat of Christmas, the feeling that this wasn't the way things were meant to be.

"She's so beautiful, isn't she?" his mother said as Kate Winslet walked onto the screen. "Those eyes. They remind me of Charlotte's eyes."

"There's something about that," Andrew agreed.

"She's really come to life since she met that Everett character," his mother said. "I can't wait to spend more time with him when he comes over from LA. I hope he stays. Your sister really needs a win after all that happened. Jason's death nearly destroyed her. When you went away, I felt like I couldn't breathe properly for weeks. I can't imagine what Charlotte went through. Jason never came back from that day of fishing. It's enough to give you nightmares."

Andrew pondered this for a long time. Finally, he said, "I'm a bit nervous to see Dad."

"It's understandable," his mother returned. "There's so much chaos between the two of you—so much unsaid."

"I don't even know if it's possible to get through it," Andrew breathed.

"Don't you want to see if you can find a way through all this pain?" his mother asked him. "Don't you want to at least try? Don't for a minute think that he doesn't love you. That he isn't partially to blame for you leaving. This is not all on you. Besides, it's Christmas time—a time for forgiveness and bringing families together once again. It's the most magical time of the year."

Deep down, he knew his mother was right. It was Christmas time and he knew he had to make things right once and for all. It was, after all, like his mother stated, the most magical time of the year.

Chapter Fifteen

Three days later, it was December 18. Already, it was seven days before Christmas, and the Montgomery family home was vibrant with holiday cheer—constantly simmering with smells of Christmas cookies and the roaring fireplace and whatever clam chowder or meat pie someone had made. Andrew stood before his childhood mirror and adjusted his button-up shirt, which he had chosen to wear for his father's pick-up. He had decided to greet his father now rather than while he was in the hospital recuperating. He didn't want to experience another PTSD episode in front of his dad. But now, his mother was exhausted, and the other siblings were occupied, so Andrew had decided to bite the bullet and pick up his father himself. It was the kind of thing a brave man would do, and he wanted to be able to tell himself he was a brave man.

And hadn't his father always wanted to raise a son who could be brave in the face of difficult things?

Andrew borrowed his mother's car. He waved goodbye to her through the kitchen window as he backed out of the driveway and into the plowed road. He was grateful that his leg remained at a dull ache, rather than a sharp pain, all the way through his drive.

When he reached the hospital, he headed toward the rehabilitation center, where his mother had told him his father would be discharged. Outside the window of the exercise area, Andrew was surprised to find that his father's rehabilitation nurse was none other than Beth Leopold.

There she stood: a woman he had very much loved as a teenager; a woman who seemed to understand the inner sadness of his soul. She spoke to Trevor Montgomery with a smile as she jotted various items onto her clipboard. His father laughed several times at what she said, as though they'd become fast friends over the course of his inpatient treatment.

Andrew remained in the hallway with his hands tucked into his pants pockets. His legs and his heart had given up on him. In the next minutes, he would say the first words he'd said to his father in years.

Beth stepped around his father's wheelchair. She turned her head toward the far end of the room, where a young boy appeared in a thick winter coat and an oversized red backpack. The boy was adorable, with a dark bowl-cut and round, curious eyes. Andrew remembered that Beth's son had autism; perhaps this was why he'd come to work with her that day.

Beth snapped her hand over the automatic door opener. Together, the three of them emerged into the drafty hallway. Andrew's eyes turned from Beth's down to his father's, where the old man looked at him with heavy sadness etched across his face. Within his father's face, he felt the question: *Can we actually fix the past?*

Instead, Trevor Montgomery's first words to his son were, "Andrew, you look just like your grandfather when he was your age. It's remarkable. You two could have been twins."

At first, Andrew wasn't sure what to say. It felt so strange to be compared to the long-gone man now, but it also felt oddly comforting to know that he had a lineage. He'd come from somewhere.

"You'll have to show me some pictures," Andrew said. "Shag and all?" He gestured to his beard.

"Shag and all," his father affirmed. "The man had an incredible beard."

"Mom asked me to shave it today," Andrew said with a laugh. "Old habits die hard with mothers."

"Seems that way," his father said good-naturedly. "The woman still worries if Steven has a warm coat or if Claire is eating enough. Sometimes it's torture. Other times, it's comforting, knowing that the limit to how much she cares for all of us doesn't exist."

Andrew nodded. After a pause, he said, "It's good to see you, Dad."

"You too, Andy."

They held one another's gaze for a long time until little Will stepped up beside his mother, gripped her hand, and said, "Mommy, do you think we could go home soon?" The words broke the spell, and both Andrew and Trevor laughed.

"Poor kid, having to deal with us all this time," Trevor said.

"Take as much time as you need," Beth said. Her cheeks brightened to crimson. "Baby, we'll stop at the burger place on the way home, okay? You've been so patient today."

"Wow. Burgers? I'm pretty jealous of that," Andrew said.

"Me too," his father affirmed.

They exchanged glances. Suddenly, the idea of being alone together seemed like the most terrifying thing in the world.

"You two can join us if you like," Beth said softly.

* * *

It was the strangest group of four in the world. Andrew pushed his father's wheelchair out onto the sidewalk that flanked the hospital. The rushing wind was cold against the tears in his eyes as they headed toward his mother's car. There, Beth assisted him in placing his father in the backseat of the vehicle before he folded up the wheelchair and put it in the trunk.

"We'll see you over there, then," Beth said as she gripped Will's hand and gave Andrew a firm nod.

"Yep. See you."

Andrew got into the driver's seat and turned to check on his father. He'd managed to buckle himself with his good arm, and he stared straight ahead, his chin lifted.

"You ready to get out of here, Dad?" Andrew asked.

"Never been more ready for anything in my life," his father returned.

At the burger place, Andrew stood in line for the three of them while his father sat in his wheelchair at a table across from Beth and Will. Will chattered excitedly about the little toys that the burger place gave out to kids, and Andrew's father asked questions as they went, which seemed to add fuel to Will's excitement. Andrew turned back to catch Beth's eye. When he did, he winked at her—something he hadn't done in years. She blushed all over again.

"New friends?" she mouthed, referring to Trevor and Will.

Andrew shrugged and grinned even wider. "Why not?"

At the counter, Andrew ordered a kid's meal, two large burger and French fry combinations for himself and his father, and chicken fingers for Beth.

When he returned to the table, they received him like he'd been gone for decades. Will jumped with excitement as he tore into the plastic wrapping around his Spiderman toy and began to tap the little figure all over the table, showing off what skills Spiderman had.

When Trevor took the first bite of his burger, he groaned with pleasure and closed his eyes. "I don't think Kerry's allowed me to have a burger this greasy in over twenty years."

Beth giggled. "I really shouldn't allow any of this to happen either. I'm your nurse, for goodness sake! But it's all in the spirit of Christmas."

"That's right. And in the spirit of reunion," Trevor said as he turned slowly toward Andrew. "I used to take you here when you were a little boy—this very one. Do you remember? You must have been five or six. I swear you went just as crazy as Will is now over those toys."

"Every time we came here, I thought I was going to lose my mind," Andrew said.

Trevor chewed thoughtfully. "Me too, you know. It was crazy to me. I'd raised all these other kids. Steve was about ready to take off for the open world. And you. You were this creative, exciting kid. You wanted to dream up stories of your future. I wasn't sure we had anything at all in common, but you made me laugh. Jeez, you made me laugh. And I loved you. More than you'll ever know. "

When they finished up and drove home, Andrew and his father sat in Kerry's car in the driveway of the Montgomery household as the snowfall doubled down around them. Inches of fluffy snowflakes bustled up on either side of the windshield; already, nearly an inch had added itself to the top of the rearview mirrors. Andrew had only just clicked off the radio, and the eerie silence filled their ears. It was essential that one of them say something. But what?

"There she is," Trevor said as Kerry pulled open the screen door and waved a hand. She called something that neither of them could hear. "I bet she's just getting her coat on to help us out. Pretty annoying, huh? All this limping around."

Andrew dropped his chin slightly. Obviously, his father had noticed his injury. "It's been quite a year."

"You can say that again."

Kerry disappeared for a moment into the dark belly of the

house. This left the men with limited time together, just the two of them.

"Maybe I'll regret saying this," Trevor offered finally. "It's certainly not something I would have told you a few years ago. I don't even think I would have had the vocabulary for it seventeen years ago. In any case, every time that phone rang in that big old house, I really did think, 'Hey. Maybe that's Andy this time. Maybe he just wants to say hi.' And you know what? It never was. Not once. But I still hoped and prayed that someday you would call."

Andrew's throat swelled with sadness. He swallowed the lump that threatened to choke him.

All Andrew could muster to say in response was, "I've been through hell and back, Dad."

Suddenly, Trevor placed his hand over Andrew's, there on the ignition. He gripped his hand hard as he closed his eyes. Whatever existed between them, it was the truest thing they could find.

"As a father, all I ever wanted was to keep you safe, Andrew. I failed you. I hope you can find a way to forgive me— to love me again. It's the only thing I want in the world."

Andrew turned to his father just then and whispered. "I love you too, Dad."

Kerry hustled out in her winter clothes. She looked frantic yet overly excited, and she yanked open the passenger side door with more strength than her seventy-one years should have allowed. She beamed down at them as she said, "There they are. Two of my three favorite men in the world."

It was surprisingly simple to get his father back in the house. Andrew placed the wheelchair tenderly beside the backseat; then, Trevor gripped the handles of the wheelchair as Andrew lifted him into it. It took nearly all his strength for just the slightest moment. Then, his father was settled, and his mother's hands latched over the back of the chair as she pushed him through the snow.

"It's really coming down, isn't it?" she said. "All things go okay up at the hospital? You're a bit later than I thought you would be."

"We had to make a pit stop," Trevor said. He turned slightly to wink up at Andrew. "With Beth Leopold and her son, Will."

His mother arched her eyebrow toward him, clearly surprised. "Oh! How funny is it that she's your father's nurse after all these years."

"And a great one, I might add," Trevor said as they slipped inside.

Upon entering, Trevor Montgomery gasped. Somehow, in the hours since Andrew's departure, his mother and his sisters had elevated the Christmas decorations and spirit in the house: more tinsel, more holly, more Christmas cookies, and more exciting flavors. On top of it all, beautiful music played softly in the background.

"It's like a Christmas wonderland," Trevor said with a laugh. "I don't know what to do with myself."

Gail and Abby appeared in the hallway with a platter of Christmas cookies. "Grandpa!" they said in unison as they stepped forward and knelt down to show him the selection.

"Girls, you made my favorite!" he said. "What a wonderful surprise. I guess I'll take a reindeer for now if you save me a Christmas tree cookie for later."

"There's enough to go around for ages," Kerry said as she slipped out of her winter coat.

"You say that now. It's still seven days till Christmas. Still plenty of time to eat up all our Christmas cookie reserves and make room in our bellies for more," Trevor said.

"I guess you're right. I should never underestimate a hungry Montgomery," Kerry said.

Andrew wheeled his father into the family room, where Steve, Kelli, Claire, Charlotte, and Rachel awaited. They all stood quickly and greeted their father with warm hugs and kisses. The conversation was chaotic. Everyone had his or her own question about the next steps of the treatment, whether or not they'd fed him well up there, and how it felt to be almost completely immortal.

"Nothing can get you down, Daddy," Kelli told him as she placed a loving kiss on his cheek.

Everyone settled back in the family room. It was the first time the entire family, all five children and their parents had been in the same room at the same time in seventeen years. A peace came over all of them as they settled deeper into their chairs. Gail got up to change the DVD to something Grandma Kerry had said she wanted to watch: *A Christmas Carol*.

After years of trouble sleeping, Andrew found his eyelids drooping. He was completely calm. That night, after his father and mother had put themselves to bed in the make-shift bedroom downstairs, Andrew collapsed in a heap on his child-hood bed and he didn't dream— not even the nightmares that normally plagued him.

Chapter Sixteen

Beth sat with her legs crossed beneath her and a thick romance novel stretched across her thigh. She hadn't managed much focus that night, not after the quick foray to the burger place with Andrew, Will, and Trevor Montgomery. She had hardly touched her chicken fingers; the nerves had gotten to her. She'd felt the tension between father and son, and she had further felt the angst between herself and Andrew. There was so much unsaid, so much that couldn't be said. All the while, Will had rattled out facts about Spiderman, enough facts to make them all laugh and have a really good time.

That was the thing about Will. He always brought people together.

Will stood from his dinosaur toys and stretched his mouth into a yawn. He blinked those beautiful eyes toward Beth as he said, "I will brush my teeth now."

That was another thing about Will. He was always very conscious of his needs. Beth, on the other hand, had neglected her needs for years. Single? Lonely? Maybe needing to eat something with some actual nutrients? She hadn't bothered with anything at all beyond taking care of Will and her other patients.

After she tucked Will in for the night, Beth enjoyed the silence of herself, her book hollow of any emotion and her eyes glassy.

Trevor Montgomery had already made good progress in her few days of working with him. He had mentioned Andrew a handful of times throughout their sessions. Mostly things like, *"I never understood him, but that doesn't mean I didn't or don't love him,"* or, *"I remember when Andrew liked you so much. He never said a word about it, but he brought you up so much in conversation that I really thought the two of you would wind up married. Time always has a different course for us, though, doesn't it?"*

"Shut up," Beth moaned to herself. She stood and emptied out the rest of her wine glass. The last thing she needed on earth was a hangover as she worked with patients the following day. Plus, she had a real goal to get Will off to school in the morning. It was the final day of the semester, the last day before Christmas break. She knew that made it a kind of fluff day. The teachers usually made cookies. The children were kinder, more genuine, and more eager. She prayed that Will would lean into the day and maybe make something of it. Sometimes, once in a blue moon, he returned home from school with an extra pep to his step.

Beth washed her face with a gentle exfoliate, added her night lotion, then slipped beneath the sheets. Outside, the snow had kept up its pattern; it flattened itself against the window-pane and then immediately melted, as the house around her was warmer than anything the outside could give her. As she drifted off into a deep sleep, her mind thought only of Andrew and Kurt, all those years ago, preparing for a Christmas in Afghanistan.

* * *

The next morning, Beth watched, triumphant, as Will slipped away from the car, stomped through the snow, and entered his elementary school without a second thought. She clapped her hands together and then noticed the long drop-off line behind her. It was time to get lost.

When she reached the hospital, she found Ellen in the breakroom.

"I heard Trevor Montgomery made it out of here," Ellen said with a smile as she adjusted the hair atop her head.

"He should be coming back in for a rehabilitation session this afternoon," Beth told her.

"And how's it been with him?"

Beth gave Ellen a secretive smile, one that Ellen almost immediately saw through. "What?" she demanded.

"What do you mean?" Beth asked.

"You look like you just thought of something but don't want to tell me," Ellen said.

"No. You know that I don't have any secrets. Just living my plain-old, boring life and waiting for my patient to arrive."

Andrew appeared outside the window of the rehabilitation center around one-thirty in the afternoon. Trevor Montgomery grinned down below him, seated in his chair, and then lifted his hand to give her a vibrant wave. She smiled and waved back.

"I see that the burger didn't kill you," she said as she pressed the automatic door button.

"In fact, I think I feel stronger than ever," Trevor told her.

"And you, Andy?"

"I ran twenty-six miles this morning," Andrew told her.

Beth chuckled a bit too loudly. "In the snow?"

"I prefer running marathons in the snow," he joked. "It builds character."

"Don't listen to him," Trevor said. "He's putting us on."

"Don't give the game away, Old Man," Andrew said, chuckling.

"Whatever," Trevor said. "We'll be done in an hour and a half or so, right, Doctor?"

"I'm no doctor, Mr. Montgomery. But I will help you get out of this chair," Beth said.

"Then let's get cracking," Trevor said.

Once the session was over, Andrew appeared back outside the window. He waited till Beth gave the all-clear before he entered. The moment the door opened, he gave them this ridiculous, cutting smile, one that made Beth weak at the knees.

"What kind of trouble did you get yourself in?" Beth asked him. She forced herself not to look into his eyes. It was too intense.

"Oh, you know. This and that," Andrew said with a wink.

"Whatever that means," Trevor affirmed. He tilted his head, then added, "You know, it's December 19, isn't it? It seems to me you kids should be out celebrating."

"Kids? Celebrating?" Beth laughed. "I don't think we're kids anymore, Mr. Montgomery. As much as I wish I was. The good old days are long gone."

"I don't know. It seems to me there's a lot here to celebrate." Trevor's eyes turned from Beth to Andrew and back again. He seemed to be trying to cook up some kind of scheme between the two of them. "Tell me you'll head out tonight together for me. Experience the nightlife. I don't think I'll catch sight of it for quite some time."

When Beth met Andrew's eyes again, her heart thudded like a wild drumbeat.

"I never did get to experience any Oak Bluffs bars," Andrew said suddenly. "I left when I was eighteen."

"They're all pretty different than they were then," Beth said.

Andrew shrugged. "Then show me. Show me what I've missed over the years."

Beth chewed at her lip. A problem arose like a cloud: she had to figure out something to do with Will.

At that moment, Ellen marched past the window. She waved a hand en route, which led to Beth bursting out of the room to ask her if she could babysit Will that evening. "Remember how I told you I've been living my plain-old, boring life?"

Ellen blinked wide eyes at her. "Yep..."

"Maybe I don't want to anymore," Beth whispered. "And I was wondering if you could help me dig my way out."

* * *

Beth piled into the passenger seat of Kerry Montgomery's car. From the back, Trevor hollered that he was hungry as heck; he hoped Kerry had gone ahead and cooked up more clam chowder. "Now that I've come back from the dead, all I want to do is eat that chowder," he told them. "I don't see much point for anything else."

Once back at the Montgomery residence, she helped prop Trevor up in his wheelchair, then hung out near the car while Andrew took him the rest of the way. From where she stood, she heard light banter between them: things like, "She looks at you like you're something special, Andy. She always has, and I guess she always will."

To this, Andrew just grumbled. Still, the whole experience was so funny to Beth that a giggle bubbled up in her stomach.

"What are you laughing about?" The voice rang out from the other side of the car. Beth whipped around to find Claire, Charlotte, and another handsome, dark-haired man whom Beth had never seen before. They all gave her curious but well-meaning smiles.

"Hey! Hello," Beth tried. Again, she felt like a foreigner in someone else's life. "They're just a couple of characters, is the reason why," Beth continued. "They made me laugh all the way home from the rehabilitation clinic."

Claire and Charlotte exchanged glances. The dark-haired man stepped forward just a bit and said, "I don't think we've met yet. My name is Everett."

"This is the guy Charlotte met when she put on that insanely expensive wedding last month. Around Thanksgiving," Claire informed her.

Beth had read something about that wedding in the papers; there had also been two alcohol poisonings from mid-tier celebrities at the hospital that weekend. One of them had been reported as saying that she "absolutely hated Ursula" and that she'd planned to go to the wedding just to tear it apart. She hadn't succeeded, obviously, since she had spent the night in detox at the hospital.

"Everett's just arrived from California," Claire informed Beth.

"That's a temperature change if I've ever heard of one," Beth said.

Everett shoved his hands in his pockets and shivered. He stepped closer to Charlotte and delivered a handsome smile. "What can I say? Something about Martha's Vineyard really caught my eye. I can't say if it was the trees or the water or the architecture."

Charlotte swatted him playfully as a blush flickered across her cheeks. "You're impossible, you know that?"

Andrew returned to the driveway. Once there, he splayed his hand across Beth's back tenderly, as though they really were that couple she'd once wanted them to be.

"Hey there," he said curiously to Everett.

"Oh, gosh, Everett. I told you all about my brother, Andrew," Charlotte said.

Everett hustled to the front of the car so that he could shake Andrew's hand properly. Andrew beamed at him as he said, "Wow, all that way from California. So glad you could make it. I hope Charlotte won't put you to work too badly. We've hustled around this place, making it all spick and span for Christmas."

"Seems like I knew exactly when to come: right after all the work is finished. It's good to meet you," Everett said.

"Where you guys off to?" Claire asked.

Andrew and Beth made eye contact again. Beth half-expected Andrew to bail, especially now that his siblings had arrived and the family was all cozied in together.

"We're headed to town to get some food and maybe a drink," Andrew told them. "We'll be back tonight."

"Okay. Just not too late," Claire said. "As Dad demonstrated, these streets can get pretty icy."

Once inside the car, Beth removed her hat and rustled her hair with a frantic hand. Andrew placed his foot tenderly on the brake as they eased backward out of the driveway. When they were pointed in the final direction, ready for whatever the night would hold for them, Andrew breathed, "I still can't believe all the changes around here. I was gone so long. I see the excitement in Charlotte's eyes, for sure. And this new guy seems spectacular. But the fact that Jason's gone? That my family is aging? That I've missed so many graduations and births and..."

Beth stretched her hand over Andy's wrist. Her thumb found his skin, the warmth of it, the softness of it. He turned his head quickly to catch her eye, and the romance sizzled between them.

Why had she touched him like that?

"You're here now. That's all that matters," she murmured as she slowly removed her hand again.

Andrew's eyes remained perplexed. For a moment, Beth

thought he actually planned to ask her to link her fingers with his. *Keep doing that.* Please. But maybe it was too much, too soon. Andrew was a bit like a frightened child who'd been through too much trauma elsewhere. She supposed she was similar.

Chapter Seventeen

Andrew parked in the makeshift lot behind the Oak Bluffs bar and grill, a place that certainly hadn't changed its décor on the outside and seemed committed to boisterous holiday drinkers, fried food, and good loud music. As they walked toward the front door, Andrew's fingers flickered against Beth's, and her eyes sparkled. Maybe if he'd been a teenager again, he would have pressed her against the side of the brick building and kissed her right there beneath the moon and stars.

The bar was pure chaos. Fryers sizzled in the back while women giggled. Men grunted over a pool table, gossip wafted through the air, and chatter seemed to be ever-present. Andrew knelt to ask Beth what kind of drink she wanted. Just before she answered, his eyes found three familiar faces toward the corner of the bar. There sat the Sheridan sisters: Christine, Susan, and Lola. Although he had only seen Christine during his brief trek back to the island, the other two were so reminiscent of his Aunt Anna that the connection was obvious.

"Do you mind if we say hi to my cousins?" he asked Beth.

Beth shook her head so that her hair danced beneath her hat. "Not at all."

Overcome with some sense of hope, Andrew strung his fingers through Beth's as he led her to the Sheridan sister's table. When they neared them, Susan, Christine, and Lola turned to deliver their sterling smiles. Susan's hair was still short, apparently from the chemo, but her eyes were as bright as ever.

"Andrew Montgomery!" Susan cried. "I never thought I would see you again. And I guess I haven't since you were, what? Seven? Eight?"

Andrew fell into a warm hug. Part of his body tricked him into the belief that this hug was one straight from Anna Sheridan herself. As he drew back, he forced himself back to reality.

"You were off on a great adventure, if I recall correctly," he said.

"The adventure is over and done with, I'm afraid," Susan said.

"That's not true," Lola interjected. "We've all created new adventures here, remember?"

"Maybe you're on one of your own," Christine said as their eyes shifted toward Beth.

"I guess you guys probably know Beth Leopold," Andrew said, speaking just loud enough to be heard over the speaker system.

"Of course we do!" Susan called. "Hey, there, Beth!"

Beth waved and said something nobody could hear. Everyone nodded and smiled as though they'd heard, which made Beth and Andrew laugh all the more. Although he loved his cousins and so wanted to catch up with them sometime, these moments were meant only for him and Beth.

"I'll see you ladies at Christmas, right?" Andrew asked.

"Actually, we wanted to talk to you about that," Susan said.

She gripped his elbow as though she knew he was on the run. "We thought we could have it at the Sunrise Cove. We could clear all the tables from the bistro and set up cozy couches. There's also the fireplace and that whole area out by the water, where we could set up a fire pit and a BBQ."

"I don't think I'm the one in charge of Christmas," Andrew said. "Although I might be able to put in a good word."

"Just think about it," Christine said. "Our family has jumped to a monstrous size these days. The Sunrise Cove is about as empty as a haunted house right now. We might as well fill it with love and both families."

Andrew nodded in agreement with his elder cousin, Susan. He really liked the idea of a Christmas dinner with both families. He told the girls he would let Kerry know, and someone would get back to them about it.

Andrew grabbed two pints from the bartender, and they headed to a circular table toward the opposite corner of his cousins, beneath an array of Christmas trees that had been hung the slightest bit crooked. Andrew lifted his glass of beer and said, "To you, Beth. Thank you for all you're doing for my dad."

Beth clinked his glass and studied his eyes for a moment.

"What?" Andrew asked, wearing a sheepish grin on his face.

"I think you've done a lot more for your dad's health than I ever could have," Beth admitted.

Andrew sipped the top foam of his beer. "I have to admit. The man seems to have lost all his hard edges over the years."

"That tends to happen to people, don't you think? You have to learn empathy sometime, even if it happens a little late in life," Beth said.

"All those years I spent overseas and in those tiny apartments in Boston, I never thought the man had it in him,"

Andrew said. "I guess it's just another example of me being wrong."

Beth swept her hand across his wrist and held it tenderly. "No. It's not that you're wrong. You just finally have a chance to rebuild your relationship. It's a chance that most people don't have. Maybe both of you sense that it's finally time."

Andrew studied her beautiful face, the way the twinkling Christmas lights reflected across her high cheekbones and highlighted the darkness of her hair. He wanted to tell her that he really hadn't wanted to leave her; he just hadn't known what to do next. Boston had seemed like the best possible option.

"I was so young and stupid when you first knew me," he tried.

"Weren't we all?" Beth returned.

Andrew shrugged. "You probably remember it, right? That first crummy apartment that Kurt and I had."

Beth scrunched her nose as she chuckled. "It was a hole in the wall, that's for sure."

"We loved it, though. We thought it was the solution to all of our problems," Andrew continued. "But when I watched you walk out the door and head back to Martha's Vineyard, I had this funny urge to run after you. I wanted to throw my arms around you and tell you not to go without us. You were headed back to the life that we were running from. After that, we completely cut ourselves off from anything associated with this island."

The conversation held onto Kurt for another full beer. Andrew hadn't really talked about his best friend since right after his death, and it was cathartic and soothing, discussing old memories with Beth, even hearing the little ways that her laugh resembled Kurt's. After a while, it was almost like Kurt sat at the bar table with them, sharing in the beers and the banter. Only almost, though.

Beth explained a bit more about Will: about the stranger

she'd had an affair with, about the pregnancy she only found out about after the stranger had left the island for good. Obviously, because Beth was Beth, she hadn't thought about anything but raising the baby herself.

"The diagnosis was, of course, hard on me," she said. "I worried that he would never be able to live his life like the other kids. But you know what? He has a heart of pure gold. I think, in some ways, his life is even more of a blessing than it might have been otherwise. Not that I could ever know."

"Did you ever try to have a—" Andrew faltered. He recognized that his question was a little forward, and he didn't want to make Beth uncomfortable.

"A relationship? Like a father figure for Will?" Beth asked.

"You're too good. You knew where I was headed."

Beth chuckled good-naturedly. "Honestly, it's mostly been me and Will, Will and me. It's been enough for a long time."

Andrew couldn't tell if this was some kind of hint that she wanted more of him or proof that he needed to back off. Still, he was captivated by her, with her laugh and her smile. As they continued their light banter on various topics, Andrew found himself leaning forward into the conversation toward her face, almost mesmerized by her smile and the way her lips moved when she spoke. He wanted more of her. They needed to make up for lost time.

What seemed like a blink later, the bartender announced that he would be closing up in ten.

"What?" Andrew and Beth said in near-unison.

"It feels like we've only been here like forty minutes or something," Andrew said. He grabbed his phone to check. It revealed 11:50.

"Oh my gosh," Beth cried. "Ellen is going to kill me." She grabbed her own phone to check for missed messages. "Huh. Nothing."

"Maybe she fell asleep at your place," Andrew suggested.

"Maybe." Beth sounded doubtful. "Can you drop me off at my house? I can have Ellen pick me up for work tomorrow."

As Andrew stood and grabbed his coat, his tongue felt like a weighted blanket across the bottom of his mouth. He needed to say something—something that translated exactly what he felt about her. Something that told her how much she'd mattered to him through the previous years.

That moment, however, had other plans for him.

His phone buzzed. In the days since his arrival, he had gotten all his siblings' numbers. The caller ID said: Kelli. His stomach soured as he lifted it to his ear. He felt sure that something was wrong.

"Kelli?"

"Andy, hey." Sure enough, her voice was strained. She sounded like she was trying to hide and not breathe or speak too loudly. "Andy, can you come pick me up? He—he hid my keys. I can't find my keys."

Chapter Eighteen

Andrew and Beth crunched through the snow frantically, tracing the path back toward the car. Once there, Andy's hand shook so hard that he dropped the keys into the white froth near the tire. He cursed to himself as he lifted them out and shook his frigid, red hand around. "That hurts," he winced.

Beth's house was only a few streets from Kelli and Mike's. He dropped Beth at the corner and apologized profusely. "I'll explain better when I see you next." Just before she drew herself completely out, he reached over and gripped her hand. "Thank you for a beautiful night, Beth. Sleep well."

"It was one of the more beautiful nights I've had in years," she told him softly as she turned back toward her house, which was dark save for the light from the television in what looked like the back room.

The moment Beth was safely latched behind her door, Andrew throttled his car as quickly as he could toward Kelli's. His lights shone across the driveway, and on cue, the side door erupted open to reveal a bundled-up Kelli. She dove into the passenger seat and snapped the door closed.

"Drive, Andy," she told him. "Just get me out of here."

That moment, Mike appeared at the side door. He remained in a t-shirt and a pair of jeans; he looked like he hadn't even put on his shoes. He waved an angry hand but made no run toward them.

Andrew was panicked and enraged. He'd never seen his sister run away from a situation like that. He placed his hand on her shoulder and said, "Kelli, I need you to answer me very carefully. Did he hurt you?"

Kelli shook her head violently as she bit into her lower lip. "No." Her voice cracked. "But for the first time in a long time, I really thought he was going to, Andy. I really thought he could have done it. He was so angry."

Andy threw himself against the side of the car. His blood boiled as he reached for the car handle. He would do it all over again. He would punch his abusive brother-in-law in the face without even batting an eyelash. He didn't care what happened to him next.

But Kelli grabbed his arm with such strength that Andrew paused. He looked into her eyes as she shook with sadness.

"Don't go after him. Don't. Lexi's in there. I don't want her to know anything about this. If we divorce, we divorce. People do that all the time. But whatever it is you want to do to him? That will scar her worse than anything else. Please. For Lexi. For me."

Andrew couldn't speak. He ran a hand through his hair as his sister's words sunk in and started to make sense. She was right. Now was not the time to deal with this. He quickly slid into his seat and pressed his foot on the gas to get them out of there. They drove back down the icy driveway, nearly losing control, then high-tailed it toward the house in which both of them had grown up.

Neither of them spoke throughout the drive. Several times, Kelli let out a hiccup that turned into a kind of wail. Andrew wanted so badly to ask her what had happened and what the fight had been about, but he could hardly get through his own anger enough to articulate his thoughts.

He pulled up in the driveway and turned the engine off. The lights dimmed around them just as more snow began to fall.

"Seems like it's always picture perfect around here," Andrew said.

Kelli snorted at that. "Yeah. Exactly picture perfect. You're so right."

Andrew allowed his shoulders to sag. He suddenly felt overwhelmingly exhausted. "Let's go in, okay? I'll cook you up something to eat. We don't have to talk. We can just be."

Kelli nodded somberly.

Kelli sat at the kitchen table in a heavy, old sweatshirt they had found in Andrew's old bedroom. Andrew hovered over the stovetop as the tea kettle heated. He rubbed his hands together and then searched through the refrigerator for something to warm up. All the while, Kelli stared straight ahead. She looked like she was somewhere else entirely.

Luckily, there was a bit of clam chowder left over. Christine had brought over another batch of freshly-baked bread, which Andrew sliced up and placed in the toaster oven. In minutes, the smells of the savory soup and toasted baguette filled the room. Their hearts calmed down as they found space to breathe again.

Just as Andrew placed a cup of hot cocoa and Baileys in front of Kelli, a light snapped on in the hallway. There was the creak of their father's wheelchair just before he appeared in the doorway. He blinked sleepy eyes before he fully recognized them and offered a smile.

"Hey there," he said. "What are you two doing up?"

"Just having a nightcap," Andrew said. After a pause, he added, "Do you want to join us?"

Trevor did. He wheeled toward the table and stationed himself beside Kelli while Andrew hurriedly filled another two cups, portioned out the toasted baguette on a platter, and filled a small bowl of heated clam chowder for Kelli. His father's eyes flickered toward Kelli for a moment with curiosity. The old man was clever enough to understand that this wasn't something you asked about. This was just something you helped carry along with you so that Kelli didn't have to bear it alone.

And assuredly, the entire Montgomery family knew the depths of Mike's horror by now.

Andrew turned on the radio. As it played softly in the corner, he joined his father and sister at the kitchen table. They clinked glasses and held the silence for a long time as they each nibbled from the clam chowder and the baguettes and sipped their hot cocoa spiked with Baileys. Each of them had something different to stew about.

The radio played an old version of "I'll Be Home for Christmas." The old recording crackled with nostalgia. Andrew couldn't help himself. He turned his eyes toward his father and said, "I really am so glad to be home for Christmas."

His father nodded. He reached across the table and gripped his son's hand. Kelli's eyes filled with tears again, too. Her hand joined theirs, and they held them there for a long time. They'd lost so much time, but here they were together.

"I don't know what we did for so long without you," Kelli told him. "We love you to pieces."

His father nodded. After a long pause, he said, "I just want to say one thing."

It was impossible to know what would be said, but either way, Andrew's heart hammered away in his chest.

"For as long as I have a roof here above us," Trevor Montgomery began, "You kids can stay under it. I don't want either of you to be around any kind of violence. Not again. Not anymore. You are both a Montgomery through and through. You hear me?"

They both nodded in agreement. A few minutes later, they finished up their drinks and placed everything in the sink. It was time they all headed for bed and got some sleep.

After Trevor returned to bed, Andrew made up the bed in what had once been Kelli's old bedroom. "No way you're sleeping on the couch," he told her, trying to make his voice light.

"Thank you, Andy," she said from the doorway. She leaned her head to the side. She looked more exhausted than he had ever seen her. Over the previous seventeen years, she'd probably grappled with countless fights with Mike, raised three children, and handled the dealings of her own boutique. It stood to reason that she finally, finally needed someone else to take care of her.

"Let me know if you need anything at all tonight," Andrew told her. "I'll sleep with one eye open, just in case."

"Don't worry about me," she told him as she crawled into bed and collapsed beneath the sheets. "I think I might sleep for the next week."

"You can't," he told her simply.

"And why not?"

"You'll miss Christmas," he said, grinning in the dark. "And you know how the Montgomery family feels about Christmas. It's the most important day of the year."

Chapter Nineteen

The next morning, Kelli remained in her bedroom for a long time. Andrew, his mother, and his father joined together in the family room to discuss what to do next.

"I don't think she should go back to that house," Andrew said firmly. "She looked so scared last night."

"I agree with you," his father said. "But I don't think we should do anything until we ask Kelli what she wants. She's a grown woman, and we have to respect her wishes."

Kerry placed a hand over Trevor's and nodded somberly. "As much as it pains me to say this, I agree. When she wakes up, we'll ask her what she wants us to do. Whether that means go pack up some bags so she can stay here for a while, or allow her to return..."

Mid-way through their conversation, the screen door that led out to the driveway banged shut. Claire's voice rang out.

"Hello! Is anyone here?"

Seconds later, she appeared in the doorway to the family

room, her smile big as she tugged off her gloves. "It smells great in here. Cinnamon rolls?"

"Should be done in about five minutes," their mother said.

Claire's brow furrowed. "You guys look very serious. Did something happen?"

Charlotte's voice came next. "Hello?"

"In here, Char!" Claire called.

Seconds later, Charlotte and Everett appeared beside Claire. For a moment, silence hovered between all of them. There was so much to explain, and yet, it wasn't really their story to tell.

"All right, everyone," Kerry said with a smile. "Why don't we gather around the table? I can feed you, and we can get this day started right."

They piled around the dining room table as Andrew helped his mother with multiple small tasks: pouring coffees and taking the cinnamon rolls out of the oven and drizzling them with the icing she'd already stirred up. As he joined the others at the table, he caught the tail-end of Charlotte's story.

"And when Everett saw all the lights in the main square, he nearly lost his mind," Charlotte said.

"I thought you guys went all-out for Christmas by Thanksgiving, but the decoration has doubled or even tripled around here," Everett affirmed.

Andrew gestured around the dining room, where still more holly had been hung, where the candles were bright red with Christmas cheer, where even the family portrait had been traded out for an old one, taken around 1996, with all of them in Christmas sweaters.

"We don't do anything halfway when it comes to Christmas," he told Everett with a laugh.

Everett swung an arm around Charlotte and cuddled her close. "I have to admit, my old cold heart has really warmed up this holiday season. Who would have thought it would happen all the way out here on this cold little rock in the Atlantic?"

"Have you given any more thought to moving out here, Everett?" Kerry asked suddenly as she dug her fork into her cinnamon roll. She asked it as though she asked about the weather.

"Mom!" Claire cried. "You can't just ask that—"

But Everett and Charlotte burst into laughter. The sound was like music.

"Actually, we just talked about it this morning," Charlotte said.

"Oh?" Their mother had never looked so excited.

"I am wrapping up a few final projects out west," Everett said. "But I think by February or so, I'll be back out here for good. Or for as long as Charlotte will have me."

Charlotte rolled her eyes playfully as she lifted her lips toward his. Their kiss was delicate and so pure.

"That's fantastic news," Andrew heard himself say.

"Made only more fantastic when you announce your plans to stay for good, too, little brother," Charlotte said.

"You Martha's Vineyard people. You're all addictive. You know that? Like your personal island touch puts people in a trance and makes them instantly move to the island," Andrew said.

"You say it like you aren't one of us," Claire said. "You fell right back into the fold just like that, as if you'd only been gone a week." She snapped her fingers and winked at him.

At that moment, Kelli appeared in the doorway. She still wore an old sweatshirt, and her hair was piled up on top of itself. She delivered a sleepy smile and waved a little hand.

"Good morning, everyone," she said groggily and rubbed at her eye.

"Good morning, Kelli!" everyone echoed back.

Claire's eyes snapped toward Andrew with curiosity. It was

clear to everyone that something was going on. Luckily, everyone played along. Andrew poured Kelli a cup of coffee and loaded up a plate with cinnamon rolls. She collapsed in the chair beside him and said, "Did I hear something about fantastic news?"

"Everett's moving here!" Kerry cried.

"Oh my gosh. That's great news," Kelli said as she sipped her coffee. "Do you think you'll miss LA?"

"Not that much," Everett said. "It's all so materialistic. Normally, I'm running around, photographing big events for celebrities, and it's all the same. Even the conversations feel the same from place to place. Plus, I can always fly out for any worthy assignments."

Kelli nodded contemplatively. "And you think we'll be a little more interesting over here?"

Everett chuckled. "You're already worlds above those people."

They continued to eat and laugh. Andrew noticed that Kelli remained bright and focused. If her mind was busy in the background with fears surrounding Mike and what she would do next, she hardly showed it.

"What's up with the flower shop today?" Kelli asked Claire as they finished up.

Claire shrugged. "I put my assistant in charge today. It seemed like a good day to stop by here and spend more time with Andy."

"Don't blame me for wanting to take a day off," Andrew teased.

"I should be thanking you! I'm still so wiped out from that wedding. I can't even imagine how you feel, Charlotte," Claire said.

"It really was destructive," Charlotte said. "Although I've agreed to help with the bits and pieces of Amanda's wedding. It's coming up, you know. January is coming so fast."

"That's right," Kelli said. "Susan seems thrilled. I know she really likes the guy."

"Chris, right? I think I met him briefly at Thanksgiving," Claire said. "He's handsome and accomplished. All the things we should want for Amanda. She's the spitting image of Anna at that age, you know. So is the other one—the pregnant one. Audrey."

"Audrey is a spitfire," Charlotte said with a laugh. "She's due pretty soon, I think maybe March or April?"

"I think that's probably why we haven't seen much of her lately," Claire said. "She's reached the really difficult pregnancy months. Although nothing was more difficult when I had twins. Remember what I looked like? I was a beached whale. And I didn't give birth till July. That was my own version of hell."

Everyone chuckled with the memory, except Andrew, of course.

When they had finished breakfast, they piled the plates in the dishwasher and then joined together in the family room. Trevor flicked through the stations while Andrew sat between Claire and Kelli on the cozy couch. Kelli seemed to fall into her own thoughts while Andrew stewed in his. After a long moment, he turned toward Claire and said, "Do you have any photos of it?"

Claire arched her brow, confused. "Of what?"

"Of when the girls were first born. I know I've missed so much of your life. I'd just like some kind of image..."

Claire's face burst into a wide grin. "Of course! This is what any mother wants—to show off pictures of her babies. You'd be surprised, I guess, how little something like that comes up." She grabbed her phone and flicked through to a folder she had created of these long-ago days. "2005 was just a few years before I got a Facebook account, so the girls were spared of me posting too much about them on the internet," she said with a laugh. "They thank their lucky stars for that."

Andrew peered at the photos. There she was, Claire, around age twenty-four: beautiful, bright-eyed, with two identical and tiny babies in her arms.

"You can imagine how tired I was in this one," she said of a photo still at the hospital. "I think I was delirious. You could have told me my name was Beyonce and I would have believed you."

Andrew laughed appreciatively as he flicked through to the next photo, which was of Charlotte holding one of the girls, with Claire beside her with the other.

"Charlotte had only just found out she was pregnant with Rachel, right?" Claire said toward Charlotte, who sat holding Everett's hand on the other side of the room.

"That's right," Charlotte affirmed. "She was born the following March. I knew when I met your girls that my girl would be their best friend."

"And you were right about that," Claire said. "The girls are inseparable, even at school. Gail and Abby even sometimes call Rachel their triplet."

It was strange, yet beautiful, for Andrew to be updated in this way. He knew that if he stuck around Martha's Vineyard, he had a great deal more to learn. He wanted to know everything about his sisters' and brother's life, about his nieces and nephews. He wanted to know about the sad days as well as the beautiful ones.

* * *

The day was one of the coziest Andrew had ever spent. There was something about it that reminded him of long-ago days when his mother had allowed him to stay home from school for a sick day, if only so they could spend time together, cooking and laughing and watching television.

Steve came around the house for lunch. He smelled just the faintest bit like the auto shop, and he brought with him freshly-baked scones that were purchased from the bakery at the Sunrise Cove Inn.

"I didn't let Christine give me them for free," he announced. "We've taken too much from her already."

Kelli bit into the corner of one and closed her eyes with pleasure. "Wow. The woman knows how to bake. It's almost sinful."

Claire and Charlotte busied themselves in making everyone grilled cheese sandwiches and tomato soup, which everyone deemed the perfect meal for such a chilly day. Kerry forced them into yet another Christmas movie while they ate together on TV trays, the same ones they'd used as kids. Despite the film going on in the background, the siblings kept up their teasing and conversation. Everett, especially, got the brunt of the conversation, as everyone was so terribly curious about him. All they'd ever known for Charlotte was Jason Hamner; was it possible that this separate being from the west coast was good enough for Charlotte?

In time, Andrew felt that although Everett was different than Jason, his goofiness and the lightness of his personality shone through. He clearly adored Charlotte and made her laugh. He planned to change his entire life for her. That was enough for Andrew.

"How was it with Beth last night, Andy?" Steve interjected suddenly.

Everyone's eyes turned toward Andrew. Claire wolf-whistled playfully.

"I guess Christine told on me?" Andrew said.

"She might have mentioned she caught you out on a date," Steven said.

"That girl is one of the sweetest people I've ever met," Trevor said.

"Well, Dad said it, so it's the law," Charlotte affirmed.

"Look at him! Our baby brother's blushing!" Claire said.

Andrew rolled his eyes. "Come on, you guys."

Everyone imitated him after that. *"Come on, you guys!"* over and over until Andrew burst into laughter.

"To answer your question," he said as he wiped the corners of his eyes, "Beth and I are just friends."

"Yeah. Right," Steven said, teasing him. "Kelli, what do you think of that?"

Kelli gave perhaps her second smile of the day. Her eyes were filled with meaning and memory. "All I want in this world is for Andy to be happy. If Beth Leopold makes him happy, then I'm all in."

Everyone nodded in unison and started various discussions once again, filling the rooms with their voices and laughter.

It wasn't until around two-thirty in the afternoon that Kelli found a slot in the conversation. Her announcement, "I wondered if you guys would head over to my place and pack up a few bags for me," led to another few seconds of confused silence.

Andrew grabbed her hand in the stunned quietness. "You know we'll do anything for you, Kelli."

"I just don't want to go over there right now," Kelli said. "I'm going to call Lexi later to explain everything. She's busy with school stuff right now, but it's her last day for the semester, so I know it's time to make her understand."

In the wake of this simple conversation, Andrew, Claire, Charlotte, and Steven stood out by Claire's car and had another brief discussion. Andrew updated them on what had happened the evening before.

"I knew they were going through a rough patch, but this makes me want to..." Steven trailed off as his hands formed fists.

"I know. But we have to respect Kelli's wishes," Andrew stated. "She just wants out. She doesn't want to mess anything up for Lexi, Josh, or Sam. They love their father, and they should be allowed to love their father. Even if we hate him."

With that, everyone agreed this was the only way.

Chapter Twenty

As they drove over to Kelli's place in Claire's car, Andrew studied the list that Kelli had written up for them about what to pack for her. According to her, Mike probably wouldn't be home yet, although his schedule was constantly changing lately.

Their plan of attack was simple: they would grab the suitcase out of the hallway closet, fill it with the items Kelli had requested, then return. They'd all decided to go together for a one-person job because they hadn't managed to agree on who could perform the task best. Plus, they just needed to be there for their sister as much as they could be.

Andrew hadn't been to Kelli's house in seventeen years. As he slid her key into the lock, flashes of how it had been came into contrast with its current state: a brand-new set of counter-tops in the kitchen, photographs of Lexi, Josh, and Sam at various ages that Andrew had missed, and an enormous televi-sion in the family room, which was just off from the kitchen.

The siblings stepped up the staircase without speaking. Andrew wasn't sure why his heart rattled so violently in his chest. He was frightened, the way he'd been as a kid watching a horror movie.

Upstairs, Claire collected the suitcase from the hall closet and led the charge toward the bedroom. There, she splayed the suitcase open while Charlotte opened the bedroom closet and began to collect jeans, t-shirts, sweaters, blouses, dresses, and shoes. Apparently, the list wasn't necessary, as Kelli's sisters, Claire and Charlotte, knew precisely what she wanted.

Steven and Andrew waited near the bedroom door. Steve palmed the back of his neck as he whispered, "I should have paid better attention to all of this. I feel like I failed her as her older brother. I hate it."

"She wouldn't want you to feel that way," Andrew returned. "Maybe she wasn't ready till now."

"It just breaks my heart to know she's been in all this pain," Steven said. "Nobody should go through that."

Just as Claire began to zip up the suitcase, there was the sound downstairs of the garage door opening. It made the house vibrate around them. Steven and Andrew locked eyes.

"He's back," Steve murmured.

"And there's no way he hasn't seen my car," Claire said.

Claire dragged the suitcase off the bed, placed the wheels on the ground, and followed after Andrew, Steven, and Charlotte. They gathered at the top of the staircase as the door between the garage and the kitchen opened. Two sets of footsteps tapped across the hardwood.

"Hello? Mom? Aunt Claire?" It was Lexi's voice.

"Shoot," Claire muttered.

None of them knew what to do. They understood that the worst part of all of this was Lexi; Kelli had wanted to remain with Mike until her graduation in the springtime if only to cushion the blow. It just wasn't possible to hold on any longer.

"Kelli?" This was Mike's voice. Maybe he had picked Lexi up from school that day.

"It's now or never," Steven muttered. He took the first step down the staircase, which creaked under his weight.

Andrew, Charlotte, and Claire followed after. Andrew turned swiftly to grab the suitcase from Claire's hands; it was too heavy for Claire. As he did, his right leg screamed with pain. Just in the nick of time, he steadied himself on the railing.

"You okay?" Claire breathed.

"Yeah. Just go ahead of me. I'll be slow, but I'll make it," Andrew told her.

When Steven reached the bottom of the stairs, he turned and waved a hand toward the kitchen.

"Steven," Mike's voice rang out ominously. "What's going on?"

"Hey, Uncle Steve," Lexi said brightly. "Are Mom and Aunt Claire with you?"

Steven palmed the back of his neck once more. "Actually, I have quite a few family members with me."

One by one, Charlotte, Claire, and Andrew lined up behind him. When Andrew reached the bottom, his eyes connected with the violent ones of Mike. He'd never hated anyone more in his life.

Lexi spotted the suitcase in Andrew's hands. "What's going on?" she asked. Her voice darkened. Nervous, she grabbed her ponytail and removed the holder. Her hair spilled out across her shoulders. "Where's Mom?"

It was clear that Mike wasn't the kind of guy to try to upset his daughter; Andrew did have to hand him that.

After a long silence, Claire said, "Your mom's at Grandma and Grandpa's."

Lexi furrowed her brow. "Why?"

Claire and Charlotte exchanged glances.

Finally, Steven said, "She needs to help Grandpa out with a few things right now. We're all pitching in after the accident."

Lexi's brow settled for a moment. This seemed almost good enough for her.

"Why didn't she come to get her own stuff?" she asked.

"It was her job to take Grandpa to his therapy today," Claire said hurriedly.

This had actually happened. At least it wasn't a full-on lie.

Mike scoffed the slightest bit as Lexi said, "Can I come back with you guys? I wanted to tell Mom what happened with my English paper. She stayed up late giving me some pointers the other day, and I got my best grade yet."

"That's fantastic," Steven said, as Claire and Charlotte both cried, "Bravo!"

Only Mike and Andrew were silent. Mike seemed helpless; clearly, he wanted to keep control over Lexi in some way, but he was outnumbered, one against four.

"Sure, honey. Grab your stuff," Claire affirmed. "I'm sure Grandpa and Grandma would love to see you, too."

Lexi hurried around them and hustled up the stairs to her bedroom. This left the four siblings and their brother-in-law face-to-face.

Finally, Steve stepped toward the front door, waved a hand, and said, "Well, good to see you, Mike. Always a pleasure." His voice was about as hard as steel.

One by one, Steven, then Charlotte, then Claire stepped out onto the front porch. This left Andrew with his limp and the suitcase. His eyes remained focused on Mike's. He just knew Mike wanted to say something.

"I should have known," Mike growled suddenly, just low enough so that his daughter didn't hear upstairs.

Andrew arched his eyebrow. "Should have known what?"

"That you would mess everything up," Mike hissed. "You were always nothing but trouble. Your father always knew it. So did your brother and sisters. We were all better off with you off the island. And now, you're just going to blow everything up for the rest of us, then take off again."

The door remained open. Claire, Charlotte, and Steven stood out in the chilly wind and watched Andrew intently. For a moment, Andrew wasn't fully sure how to respond. He could have gone his previous routes—punched the guy in the mouth, that kind of thing. But it just wasn't worth it anymore.

He was so past that mentality.

"Mike, since I saw you last, I have been all over the world. I have seen so, so many people hurt and killed—countless bodies. I have buried good friends, and I have had to acknowledge some of the horrors of the universe. But beyond all that, what you do to my sister is too much for me to handle. I hope I never have to see your pathetic face again."

Andrew turned on his heel and stepped into the blistering wind. The moment he joined the others, Lexi appeared at the top of the staircase and hollered, "I'm ready!" Her voice was vibrant and alive. She hadn't heard a thing of what Andrew had said.

Andrew was grateful for that.

When they arrived at the house, Andrew noticed that Kelli was patiently waiting for them. Her cheeks were blotchy, and her eyes were brimming with tears. Lexi rushed toward her, her face panicked. "Mom, are you okay? What's wrong?"

"Thank you guys for doing that for me," Kelli said to her siblings. "It means the world."

She then drew her arm around her daughter and led her upstairs to the bedroom she'd once had as a rock-music-playing teenager. Up there, there was the sound of the door clicking closed. All the siblings knew that it was time for Kelli to explain that she planned to leave Mike for good.

It was one of the heaviest moments of their lives.

Kerry walked into the kitchen. Her face had lost all its

coloring as she said, "I'm going to get dinner started. Would you girls like to help?"

"Let me call up Rachel and Everett," Charlotte said. "That is if you don't mind having a few extra mouths to feed."

"The more, the merrier, and you know that," Kerry affirmed. "Claire, get Russel and the girls over here. And Steve, if you can wrangle your family over here, I'd love that too. You know how I feel about my great-grandbabies. I lose my mind for them." She then directed her gaze toward Andrew, who still held onto the suitcase with red-tinged, bone-cold hands. "Your father's physical therapy is about to finish up. Do you mind heading over there to pick him up?"

* * *

Andrew stood outside that now-familiar window and watched as Beth and his father facilitated the last movements of his physical therapy for the afternoon. As Beth discussed his father's pain limitations, she caught sight of Andrew and waved her hand to beckon him in.

"Hey there," she said brightly. "I hope everything was okay last night."

"It is now," Andrew said. "How was it today?"

"Just as difficult as ever," his father said. "It's going to be a long road ahead, but as I already told Beth, I know that the journey is worth its weight."

Andrew found his first smile of the day as he stepped around to grab his father's coat from the coat rack. "Always an optimist," he said of his father. "I love it."

Beth donned her own jacket and said, "I'd better run off and pick up Will. I hate leaving him with the babysitter, but they're all finished for the semester, and I still have several more rehabilitation appointments before Christmas."

"Does he like his babysitter?" Andrew asked.

"He loves her," she said with a laugh. "She studied archaeology in college, and so she just gives him random fact after random fact about some of his favorite things. Sometimes, I have to drag him out of there. What good am I, a mother without any new facts about dinosaurs?"

"I think you probably have your own things to offer him," Andrew said with a laugh.

"Shelter and food, I guess." Beth giggled.

Andrew's heart again found his throat. He could have stared into her eyes for the rest of his life.

"Beth, I don't know if you and Will have plans for Christmas," he said suddenly.

His father, of course, took this moment to interject. "Ask her to come to our Christmas gathering!"

"I think we're going to have a big one with all the Montgomerys and the Sheridans together," Andrew said. "At the Sunrise Cove Inn. Maybe, if you and Will aren't too busy, you can come by? I mean, I still remember that last Christmas with Kurt overseas. It was such a beautiful day. We tried our best to recreate the magic we used to feel at Christmas. You know? And anyway, I would love to have you there with us. I feel like you belong to the Montgomery family."

Beth's voice was so quiet when she answered.

"I only want to belong to the Montgomery family."

Back in the car, Trevor Montgomery splayed his hand out toward Andrew. His eyes shone with excitement.

"What?" Andrew asked sheepishly.

"Come on, son. Give me a high five. What you did in there? Asking Beth to Christmas? It was slick."

Andrew rolled his eyes as an easy laugh erupted from his throat. "Come on, Dad. Don't make it weird."

"As your father, it's my legal right to make it weird," Trevor said. "And I will continue to make it weird, up till your wedding day, and when your first child is born, and on and on, as long as I can. I lived through this car accident for a reason, you know. I have to believe it's because embarrassing you is my new life's work."

Chapter Twenty-One

It was Ellen who dared her to do it: *Text Andy. Ask him to go with you. You know he'll say yes.*

On Christmas Eve, Beth drummed up the courage to do exactly what Ellen said. Her heart was all over the place; her mind whirled around and around like a Ferris wheel. In the minutes while she awaited his text in response, she felt so crazy that she thought about throwing her phone out the window.

"Mom! Mom?" Will hustled in from the family room with one of his dinosaurs in hand. He beamed at her from under his bowl cut as he said, "When do you think Santa gets started today? Probably early, right? Because there are so many countries ahead of us? I just did the math. It's already tomorrow in Australia. Which means maybe he's already been hard at work for hours."

Again, Beth was mesmerized by her son's incredible mind. "I think you're right, Bud. Although, to be fair, Santa does have a pretty cushy life for the rest of the year. He lets his elves make his toys, and then he works for twenty-four hours straight, one day per year. I wish I had that kind of life."

"I think he probably has to take a lot of meetings with the elves to design the toys," Will said. "There's no way he treats them like slaves. He's Santa, for goodness sake."

Beth chuckled. For a moment, she actually forgot about the message she awaited. When the phone buzzed on the counter, she glanced at the name, and nerves shot through her like electricity.

ANDREW: I'd love to go. What time?

* * *

It had become a tradition before her parents passed away. Each year after Kurt's death, they would spend some time at his grave on Christmas Eve, where they told him stories about the year, about what they missed most about him, about what had gone on in the world, somehow, without him. Now, his grave had two neighbors: their parents. Beth made sure to visit them, too.

Will's babysitter arrived just as Andrew's car pulled up in the driveway. Will was a frequent visitor to the gravesite, but there was something about this night in particular that meant she and Andrew had to see Kurt's grave alone.

"Hey, Denise," Beth said in greeting. "Thanks so much for doing this. I promise we won't be gone long."

"Denise! Come check out my excavation site!" Will called out from the living room.

Denise chewed her gum as she grinned. "Don't worry about it, Beth. You know how I love my Will time." She raised her voice to call out, "I hope you secured the site so that tourists can't walk through, William!" as she disappeared into the family room.

When Beth reached Andrew's car, she was dizzy with fear, excitement and, of course, the sadness that came with visiting your family's gravesite. When she sat herself down in the passenger seat and found Andrew's eyes, she felt a wave of calm come over her.

"You look nice," she said softly.

Andrew glanced down at his suit jacket and tie. "I just wanted to dress up for him. I don't know why. I guess because I imagined him saying something sarcastic, like, 'So glad you made such a great effort, Andy,' if I came in jeans and a sweatshirt."

Beth laughed almost too long at that. "I can hear him saying that. He was hilarious, wasn't he? I sometimes tell him little jokes in my head. The ones I know he would understand."

They drove to the graveyard in silence. On the way, they passed by countless houses decorated with Christmas cheer: bright yellow and red and green lights that twinkled joyously. When they paused for the light near downtown, they heard the sound of a caroling group, only about a half-football field away. Beth opened her window, despite the chill of the air, to allow the music to fall through the crack.

Christmas time is here.

Happiness and cheer.

Fun for all that children call

Their favorite time of the year.

"Why is it that so many Christmas songs sound so sad to me?" Andrew asked with a dry laugh.

"They do to me, too. I just think Christmas is a time to remember everyone you've ever loved and create new memories with the ones you have close to you now. There's always a shadow to it. But it doesn't mean it's a bad thing." After a pause, Beth added, "Especially this year, I suppose."

Andrew nodded. "I have to agree with you there."

Andrew parked outside the graveyard as the sun began to flicker beneath the horizon line. Slowly, they got out of the car and met at the front hood, where they instinctively held hands before heading the rest of the way toward the fence.

When they reached Kurt's grave, Andrew's thumb traced a delicate motion over the palm of her hand. "There it is," he murmured. "Kurt Henry Leopold. 1985 to 2005. He's been gone so, so long, now. But you're right. I can still hear his voice in my head."

Beth squeezed his hand a little bit harder as a tear trickled down her cheek. Softly, she said, "Kurt, I wanted to tell you that Will still talks about you all the time. He never knew you in real life, but I tell him so many stories that have made him fascinated. We have photos of you everywhere, so, in some ways, you're just as real as anyone else Will knows. He lives so much in his head all the time. You were like that, too, a little bit, especially when we were younger—always so shy. But you were always just waiting for the right people to be yourself around. Like me. Like Andy."

Andrew heaved a sigh. "You remember how I used to tell you, Kurt, how great your sister was? I'm surprised to say that, even though I was wrong about almost everything else back then, I wasn't wrong about that. I've missed you, buddy. I've missed all the optimism we shared together back when we wanted to go out and conquer the world. I hope you're proud of me up there. I hope you'd say something like, 'You were too stubborn. I'm glad you got over all that.' I hope you know how much we wish you were here with us. Love you, man."

"Love you, Kurt," Beth whispered. She dropped forward and traced a finger over the top of the grave.

About a half-hour later, Andrew and Beth walked along the water near the ferry docks. The Christmas lights reflected from their eyes and their bright red cheeks, and they found ways to laugh and share stories and fall deeper into whatever it was they were building. Was it love? Beth didn't know. She'd never really experienced true love yet. She hoped it was.

As they stood beside the empty ferry boats, parked for the night and for the holiday, Andrew reached out and grabbed her. Then in one fluid motion, he pressed his lips against hers. Safe in his warm embrace, Beth allowed herself to forget all the traumas of her life. She knew only the warmth and the softness of his lips; she knew only the tilt of her body against his as he traced his tongue across hers; she knew only that whatever this was, she wanted more of it. It made her weak in all the right ways.

When their kiss broke, Beth touched her lip with a finger and looked up at Andrew. Her cheeks were flushed as she said, "I swear to God you know how to steal a girl's heart."

Andrew smiled as he looked down at her and said, "I've been waiting seventeen years to do that." He pulled her into his embrace as they started walking back to their vehicle.

* * *

They arrived back at her place later to relieve the babysitter. Denise was up to her ears in dinosaurs and fake archaeology equipment.

"Absolutely, Santa was around during the dinosaurs," she said matter-of-factly. "How do you think he designed these beautiful toys? He knew them. He was even friends with some of them."

Will looked at her, bug-eyed. "That makes sense," he said.

"Hey there," Denise said. She hopped up from her position at the archeological site and swept her hands over her jeans. Her eyes turned curiously toward Andrew, who Beth hadn't mentioned anything about. "Merry Christmas Eve!" she said to him brightly.

"Merry Christmas Eve," Andrew returned. "My name is Andy. Andy Montgomery."

"I'm Denise, the babysitter," Denise said, her grin widening. "How is it out there? Freezing, I bet?"

"Would you want it any other way on Christmas Eve?" Andrew asked.

"Of course not," Denise said as she draped her coat over her shoulders. "I only dream of white Christmases."

"That's another sad Christmas song," Andrew said to Beth as Denise bid them goodbye. "I swear, every single one is like that."

Will had only met Andrew the one time after Andrew's father's rehabilitation session. As he was Will Leopold and only Will Leopold, he recognized Andrew immediately.

"I remember you. Andy, right?"

"That's right. And you're Will," Andrew said. He reached out to shake Beth's son's hand, expressing the urgency and respect he felt for the young boy. "It's good to see you again, especially on such a special occasion."

"You too. I hope you know that you have to sleep through the night to make sure Santa comes," Will informed him. "It's a part of the rules."

Andrew nodded somberly. Beth was so grateful she didn't have to explain to Andrew that you had to take Will at face value. You couldn't make fun of him; you couldn't think what he said was overly silly. His emotion and his compassion were both unparalleled.

Beth suggested that they play a game together, the three of them, before they put out the milk and cookies and went to sleep. Will changed into his Christmas pajamas, which were covered in reindeer, and burrowed himself under a blanket while Andrew assembled the board game Will picked, which was Sorry. Together, they teased one another and play-bickered as they went through the game, which, luckily, resulted in Will defeating both Andrew and Beth.

"Wow. You're good at this," Andrew told Will as he gathered up the game.

"I know," Will said. "I've never lost."

Andrew checked with Beth, who nodded. "I've never seen him lose in my life."

"It's all about strategy," Will explained. "You'd have to play as much as me to get it."

Once Will was off to bed and fast asleep, Beth found Andrew at the edge of the couch, with his hands clasped across his lap. He leaned forward slightly, as though he prepared to leave. Only then did Beth fully realize how much she wanted him to stay the night.

Was that really a good idea?

Could she really get away with this?

What would Will say if he saw him the following morning?

Andrew's smile told her everything she needed to know: he would stay if she allowed him to. He wanted this if she did.

"Will's such a great kid," he told her.

Her heart felt like a cracked egg. She collapsed beside him and again laced her fingers through his. "I can tell he really likes you. He's still testing you, of course, but all signs point to good things."

"That's a relief," Andrew said. "I know this was kind of an audition, wasn't it? And on Christmas Eve of all nights. Pretty cruel of you."

Beth laughed at the joke. "I know. But you passed with flying colors. Which means I think you deserve a glass of wine? If you want one, that is."

"Only if I can have a cookie along with it," Andrew said with a wink.

"I don't know. Is your name Santa Claus?"

Before he could answer, Beth rose, grabbed a bottle of merlot from her wine shelf, and placed two frosted cookies on a little Christmas plate. They were in the shape of bells.

When she returned, she said, "I don't think that 'Silver Bells' song is that sad."

Andrew considered this as he lifted his Christmas cookie. "City sidewalks. Busy sidewalks. Dressed in holiday style."

"In the air, there's a feeling of Christmas," Beth continued.

"Children laughing, people passing—meeting smile after smile," he said.

"And on every street corner, you'll hear..." Beth sang this time.

"I guess it's not so, so sad," Andrew agreed. "But any time you have children smiling in songs, you think of your own childhood and you want it back. All that magic."

"Which is why I'm grateful for Will," Beth said. "He keeps the magic alive for me."

Andrew looked overwhelmed. He sat his glass of wine on the coffee table, added the platter of cookies beside it, and then moved forward to kiss her again. This time, the kiss was more urgent. Their bodies seemed to call out to one another.

"Before we go to sleep..." Beth said softly, breaking the kiss, "I have to put Will's presents under the tree."

Andrew helped her every step of the way. They carried the packages up from the basement and placed them beautifully beneath the Christmas tree. They then filled the stocking—both hers and Will's. On instinct, Beth grabbed a little grocery sack and filled it with a few pieces of candy and a spare book she hadn't read yet from her bookshelf.

"What's that?" Andrew asked.

"It's your stocking," she said. "Will wouldn't forgive Santa if he thought he forgot you on Christmas."

"That reminds me," Andrew said. Hurriedly, he grabbed his keys and rushed into the night to retrieve something from his car. When he returned, he held two bright red packages.

"What are those?" Beth whispered. Her knees were on the verge of giving out.

"This one is for Will to open, from me. Something of a manipulation tactic," Andrew said with a funny smile. "And the other one? Well. You'll just have to open it tomorrow."

Later that night, giggly and much happier than she'd been in a long, long time, Beth collapsed in the arms of Andrew Montgomery. She was warm. She was safe. And tomorrow was Christmas.

Chapter Twenty-Two

The Sunrise Cove Inn looked like a postcard.

It seemed that someone—maybe God himself, or maybe just Santa Claus—had arranged the snow beautifully so that it lined the windows and the shutters and the various rooftops of the multi-generational inn just perfectly. Andrew stood with his hand wrapped around Beth's waist and with little Will all bundled up on the other side of her. Even from where they stood, they could hear the mass chaos from within.

It was a Montgomery and a Sheridan Christmas.

"We've had such quiet Christmases over the years," Beth said as they walked toward the front door. "I can't imagine how different this will be."

When they stepped into the foyer, they found themselves in the midst of an all-out party, only the kind the Sheridan sisters and the Montgomery clan could stitch together. It looked like a picture out of Martha Stewart's Christmas magazine itself, with a large tree in the corner, fully decorated and lit up.

Lola whipped forward, her long hair flowing behind her and her hand latched through the fingers of a dark-haired and handsome, broad-shouldered man.

"Andy! You made it!" She threw her arms around him and then gestured back toward her boyfriend. "This is Tommy Gasbarro. We met this year when I traveled by sailboat with him from the Florida Keys to Martha's Vineyard."

"Wow. That's incredible. I had no idea you knew how to sail, Lola," Andrew said.

Lola giggled lightly as she added, "Tommy would say that I don't know a thing, and he would be right. And if I'm honest with you, the whole expedition wasn't without its problems. We had a huge storm during the trip that made me more than a little queasy. The clouds were black as night, and I thought for sure we would go under."

Tommy rolled his eyes as he said, "Nice to meet you, Andy. And if you know Lola at all, you know she's being dramatic right now."

Tommy turned his chin down to dot a kiss on her forehead. Lola's smile grew infectious.

"And Beth! And Will! Goodness, welcome to the Sunrise Cove," Lola continued. "Let me take your coats. Susan put me in charge of them, but she really shouldn't have. I keep getting distracted."

Beth, Andrew, and Will removed their coats and watched as Lola disappeared into the back coatroom. Kerry called to them from inside the Bistro, which they could see down the hallway from the foyer.

"Come on in, guys! The fireplace is warm," she said.

Tommy, Lola, Beth, Andy, and Will entered the bistro area to see it completely re-done for a perfect family Christmas. Long tables had been set up toward the far end of the room. They were piled high with Christmas snacks—cookies and pies and delicious finger foods, that kind of thing. According to

Christine, who whipped past with a wide grin, "Christmas dinner is at one!" This was only an hour away.

"Who's cooking Christmas dinner?" Andrew asked as he, Beth, and Will sat near his mom by the crackling fire.

"Christine's boyfriend is a master chef. His name is Zach," his mother affirmed. "He also catered that wedding that Charlotte did. He's a master."

Over the next hour or so, Andrew and Beth fell into a flurry of beautiful conversations. All the while, Will sat by the fire with a few other kids, coloring in coloring books and discussing the toys they had gotten under the tree that morning. Naturally, Will's toys had taken on a dinosaur theme.

"What beautiful earrings!" Amanda, Susan's daughter, said to Beth as they spoke toward the Bistro windows, all of them with wine glasses in hand.

"Oh, thank you," Beth said as she touched the diamond rings delicately. "They were under the Christmas tree this morning, if you can believe it."

"Oh, wow. Santa really is so generous," Amanda said as she gave Andrew a bright smile.

Beside her, Amanda's fiancé shifted his weight anxiously. Andrew wanted to ask him what the heck he was nervous about. Wasn't all the wine, food, and company in the world enough for him?

"I'm going to run to the bathroom, babe," Chris said as he nodded to Beth and Andrew. "I'll grab you another glass of wine when I get out."

When Chris disappeared, Andrew said, "I heard you have a wedding coming up real soon."

Amanda blushed. "We want to get it done sooner rather than later. My career is about to become insane, and his already is. We're thinking, get the wedding done now, and then have the honeymoon later on. Summertime, when we can actually enjoy ourselves."

"That's smart," Beth said.

Amanda blushed. "I hope so. Hard to believe this is my last Christmas as a single woman."

Beth gave Andrew a funny look after that. Somewhere, in the pit of his stomach, Andrew wondered if he, too, would be married sometime soon. He hadn't envisioned that kind of life for himself, at least, not for a long time.

And the thought filled him with much more hope than he could have imagined.

"Everyone!" Christine called. "We've set up the dining table, and Zach says he's ready to serve. He's slaved away at this beautiful meal."

"I had some help," Zach said. He reached over and drew his hand around Christine's hip so that he could tug her into him and kiss her on the cheek.

"Wonderful!" Uncle Wes called. "Thank you so much!"

"Oh, and don't forget. Aunt Kerry was kind enough to cook us up a huge vat of clam chowder," Christine said. "If you grew up in the Sheridan or Montgomery family, then you know as well as I do how addicting that stuff is. I went years and years without having it at Christmas, and I always thought about it. I missed it. And I think I speak for me, Lola, Susan—and probably Andy Montgomery when I say that I missed all of you, as well."

Everyone's eyes turned toward Andrew. He blushed and lifted his hand as he said, "It's wonderful to be here." His voice was a little too soft, proof of how shy he felt. But the smiles he received back were so wholesome. He really could have flown away.

Andrew slipped his fingers through Beth's as they walked toward the beautifully decorated, incredibly long dining room table located beneath a gorgeous chandelier in the foyer. The foyer had a gorgeous view of the frigid Vineyard Sound. Andrew remembered being a little kid in that very foyer and gazing out the window. There was always something about looking out across the waters. It had always filled him with so much calm.

He'd thought of that several times when stationed overseas. The desert had served as a kind of ocean, but his heart had been entirely too black to really bring any kind of romance to the equation.

The meal was elaborate. Lola, who sat across the table from Andrew, Beth, and Will, laughed and said, "Zach always has to go all-in on dinner, doesn't he?" It was roasted ham, roasted turkey, stuffing, mashed potatoes—both regular and sweet—along with Brussels sprouts, perfectly seasoned cranberry sauce, and countless varieties of bread, including French baguettes, traditional dinner rolls, and enough scones to feed a small country. "Of course, Christine supplied the carbs," Lola teased.

Christine laughed as she passed a tray of scones down the long row of people. "You know you love it, Lola."

Beside Lola sat Audrey, a beautiful girl with a very pregnant belly. She splayed her hand over it as she directed her eyes toward Andrew and said, "This is what I've been dreaming about for months. Christmas dinner." She leaned toward him conspiratorially and said, "You can't imagine how hungry I am. I wake up every morning and feel like I could eat at least this much food. Maybe even more."

"I remember that," Beth said with a laugh as she spooned herself some Brussels sprouts. "I remember one particular day of intense cravings. I went to that diner near the airport."

"The Right Fork?" Lola said.

"That's the one!" Beth affirmed. "And I think I ate a big breakfast, read a bit of my book, and then ordered a big lunch after that. The woman working didn't bat an eye. I loved her for it."

Mid-way through dinner, Andrew caught Kelli's eye. She

was seated several seats away, between Lexi and Josh. Sam sat on Josh's other side. She looked strangely depleted; her cheeks were hollowed out, and what she'd chosen to wear wasn't exactly up to her normal "fashion sense."

Andrew mouthed to her, "Are you okay?"

Kelli nodded and tried out a smile, but it barely managed to shine through her eyes. Over the previous days, she'd had to explain the separation to her children. There had been a great number of tears spilled at the Montgomery residence, but Kelli had reported that all in all, they'd taken it with empathy and understanding.

"I guess that means you raised them right," Andrew had told her at the time.

There were round after round of toasts, almost as though the Montgomerys and the Sheridans had too much to be thankful for.

There was Susan, standing upright with her glass raised toward Amanda and Chris as she said, "I look so forward to my daughter's wedding next month. Chris, welcome to our crazy but loving family. We're so grateful for you."

Then, there was Uncle Wes, who stood and lifted his glass to his three girls as he said, "I can't believe how lucky I am to have you all back. Our house has never been more joyous. I just adore you all and the life you've given me. I hope for many more Christmases, just like this one."

Christine stood after that. "I imagine all of you are getting pretty sick of my speeches, but I have one final thing to say: Audrey, my shining and beautiful niece. You are about to become a mother, and you've allowed me the challenge and the light of helping you raise your child. I cannot wait to see what next year will bring. I imagine that next year at Christmas, things will be a great deal different. I wouldn't want it any other way."

Audrey, who seemed to normally be the kind of girl who

liked to be smarter than her own emotions, blinked back tears. She lifted her glass of sparkling water and said, "Thank you, Christine. I imagine it will be a lot louder. That's for sure."

Just when Andrew thought that the toasts were finished and separate conversations began to bubble up again, he watched as his father clinked his glass with a fork to get everyone's attention, as he couldn't stand.

"I'll add my two cents before we get back to this beautiful meal," Trevor said. His eyes scanned over, from Steve to Kelli, to Claire, to Charlotte, before they finally settled on Andrew. "As all of you know, I've had something of a pretty crazy December."

A few people chuckled knowingly and nodded. Andrew's heart nearly stopped beating.

"When I first woke up in that hospital room, and my Kerry told me my youngest son had returned home, I thought maybe I was still unconscious and having some kind of dream," Trevor continued. "But when they finally let me out, there he was. My Andrew. My Andy. He drove me home from the hospital. But I have to say, a long time ago, I made some pretty serious mistakes. I know we all have in our own way. But since he's returned, I have gotten to know the man he has become, the man I am so proud to call my son. Andrew, I'm so happy you are home; we all are. I love you, son."

Here, he held up a finger to indicate he wasn't finished and glanced toward Uncle Wes and the Sheridan sisters, who'd all experienced their own heavy truths that year.

"In any case, this toast isn't just directed toward Andrew. It's for my wife, my beautiful children, my grandchildren, and my great-grandchildren. It's also for everyone else here. As someone who nearly left this world only a few weeks ago, I have to say there's a great deal here to stick around here for. Thank you, everyone. God bless you, and Merry Christmas."

Everyone applauded his speech. Andrew wiped his tears

away the minute they fell onto his cheeks. Beth reached over and squeezed his hand hard.

"You okay?" she whispered.

Andrew nodded yes, although, in truth, he felt like a boulder had just crashed into his chest.

* * *

After dinner, everyone gathered back in the bistro area for more drinks, pie, cookies, and conversation. Audrey stationed herself toward the back, where she played Christmas songs from the speaker system. Amanda padded up and sat alongside her. The two girls were almost identical and clearly had built up a beautiful friendship in the months since they'd met.

Andrew sat near the fire, with Beth on one side, Kelli on the other, and Will stationed on the floor with another coloring book.

Suddenly, Lexi, Josh, and Sam appeared before their mother. They looked a bit awkward. They glanced at one another as though one of them was supposed to start speaking first.

"Hey guys," Kelli said. Her voice was strained. "Did you have a good Christmas dinner?"

"It was just weird for us this morning," Sam told her. "Not being together as a family."

"We weren't sure when to give you your present," Josh said.

Lexi brought out a little jewelry box from behind her back. She placed it tenderly in her mother's hand. "Merry Christmas, Mom. We're so thankful for you. And we're thankful that—" She paused for a long moment before adding, "We're thankful that you are going to find a way to be happy. We only want you to be happy."

Kelli swallowed the lump in her throat. With quivering hands, she opened the box to reveal a beautiful gold necklace with a shimmering center made of diamonds. She lifted it into the light, breathless.

"You guys," she whispered. "This is beautiful. I don't even know what to say."

"You don't have to say anything," Josh told her.

Kelli stood and hugged each of her kids for a long time. Her cheeks were lined with tears as she turned and asked Lexi to latch the back. When she collapsed back in the chair, her children's eyes remained on her. Sheepish, she said, "Did you guys get any pie? Christine's apple pie is to die for."

"Want us to grab you a piece?" Sam asked.

"That would be great, guys," Kelli said. "Thank you."

As her kids walked toward the dessert table, Kelli turned her eyes toward Andrew. She held onto the diamonds of the necklace and heaved a sigh.

"I probably look like a complete mess to you, don't I?" she asked. Her laughter was the saddest thing Andrew had ever heard.

"You've been through a lot," Andrew said.

Kelli shrugged. She leaned toward him, her voice soft, as she said, "You know, when I woke up at Mom and Dad's this morning, all I could remember were the good times. Christmases that Mike and I spent together with the kids. I couldn't remember the fights anymore. I couldn't remember why I left. But when I had that first cup of coffee with Mom around the tree, the images came crashing down again. He put me through so much. But I still find myself missing him. And I guess that might be my reality for a long, long time."

"You deserve to carve out space for a different kind of happiness," Andrew said. "But it doesn't mean you can't hold the good times close."

Kelli reached out and held onto Andrew's hand for a long time. Again, she said, "I love you, baby brother. More than you could ever know."

As more tears traced down her cheek, Will blinked up and caught sight of her. Immediately, he dropped his crayon and said, "Are you all right, Kelli?"

Andrew was shocked that Will remembered her name. He'd been introduced in passing. What else could that kid's mind do?

"I think so, Will," Kelli returned.

Suddenly, Will stood and marched toward her. His little, eight-year-old arms wrapped around her, and he placed his chin on her shoulder. The hug was so genuine and such a surprise that Andrew, again, stopped breathing. Kelli's eyes closed as she hugged him back.

They were two people on the outside of so much: Will in his autism and Kelli in her grief.

At that moment, they needed one another.

And somehow, Will had known just what to do.

Chapter Twenty-Three

That night, Kelli, Andrew, and Trevor sat around the kitchen table. The clock ticked itself toward eleven, and their bellies swelled to account for the massive feast, the pie slices, and the wine. Still, there was a platter of Christmas cookies in front of them, and they nibbled slowly as they sipped the last of their wine. There was something about the magic of Christmas. You had to see it through to midnight.

"I still can't believe Will's hug this afternoon," Kelli said softly. "I don't think I've ever felt such tenderness from a child before. When my babies were eight, they were playing in the dirt and coming up with new ways to insult each other."

Trevor chuckled. "That's not totally true, you know. Your kids were kind, considerate, and creative."

"They once threw dirt at me when I told them to come in for dinner," Kelli countered.

Both Trevor and Andrew laughed raucously.

"Well, you'd never know that, now," Andrew said.

"I guess they grew into themselves," Kelli affirmed.

"Beth spoke to me quite a bit about Will," Trevor said. "She mentioned that he understands the depth of emotion a bit differently than other kids because of his autism. Normally, people think that autistic people don't experience emotion, but it's just not true. Maybe he couldn't have translated what you were going through using words. But he saw it all over your face, and he knew exactly what to do."

Kelli nodded contemplatively. "I'll remember that hug for the rest of my life."

"That Beth really knows what she's doing," Trevor said. "I think she's had a lonely life, but she hasn't let Will know that. She's given him so much."

"And even this afternoon, I heard him telling one of the kids about you," Kelli said, her eyes pointed toward Andrew.

"What? What could he have said?"

"He talked endlessly about the toy you got him," she said with a laugh. "He said that between Santa and Andrew, he wasn't sure who was better at gift-giving. I'm trying to remember his exact words, but it was something like: 'I guess I'll have to tell Santa that his were better, but that might be a white lie. It's his job, and I don't want him to feel disheartened about his career.'"

Both Trevor and Andrew laughed outrageously at that.

"He's such a sweet kid," Andrew said. "I count myself lucky to have met him."

"I have a feeling this meeting will lead to many, many more," Kelli said with a crooked smile.

"Don't jinx me," Andrew said, although his heart ballooned with it: the knowledge that she was right.

He and Beth were on a journey now.

And Will was on that journey, right alongside them.

He wouldn't have had it any other way.

* * *

After another cookie, Kelli bid Trevor and Andrew goodnight and padded upstairs to her childhood bedroom. This left father and son in a silence that was much different than the silences of seventeen years ago. It was a silence of comfort and under-standing. It was a silence of forgiveness.

Finally, Andrew spoke.

"Maybe I really needed all that time away to see what I had left behind. Right now, it feels like none of that other life really existed. I was born on Martha's Vineyard, and maybe I want to stay."

Trevor's eyes were bright with happiness. He dropped his chin to his chest as he heaved a final sigh.

"I've never appreciated my life, or my wife, or my children more than I do right now. I know I went on and on about it in my toast, but it's true. I keep looking at this house, at all your mother and I have built together, and also at you—my son—a son who went off and fought for our nation. A son who has so much empathy and understanding, that a boy with autism immediately sees him and loves him like the role model he is. Andrew, I can't thank you enough for coming home and forgiving me. I was such a damn stubborn fool."

Andrew's eyes welled up with tears. Immediately, he reached for a napkin and dabbed at his eyes. Long ago, his father had chided him for crying; it wasn't something men were meant to do.

But suddenly, his dad's hand stretched over his. His eyes were urgent.

"Don't," he said.

"What do you mean?" Again, Andrew worried he'd done something wrong.

"Don't dry your eyes," Trevor said. "If there's anything I've learned in my old age, it's that crying is sometimes the only thing you can do. It's more than necessary. It clears out the old to make way for the new. And, with all the goodness we have in our family, there is so much new coming our way. You can bet on that."

* * *

As Andrew settled into his bed for the night, a text came in from Beth.

> BETH: Will won't sleep. He thinks your family is full of magic. I can't understand it. Normally, he gets a bit panicked in groups he doesn't understand. With yours, he fell in love.

> ANDREW: We fell in love with him, too. Kelli couldn't shut up about him.

> BETH: I hope she finds a way through this. She's such a kind, good-hearted soul.

Outside, a Christmas moon hung low in the sky. It seemed to twinkle out the wisdom of its centuries of overseeing Martha's Vineyard and all the tiny people who lived and loved there.

> BETH: Will just asked me what he should call you. That is if you're sticking around the Vineyard.

Andrew's smile was enormous in the dark.

> ANDREW: Oh, I'm not going anywhere any time soon. Tell him to call me Andy. Everyone else does.

> BETH: Andy. Andy Montgomery. That rascal. I've missed him so.

* * *

Next in the series

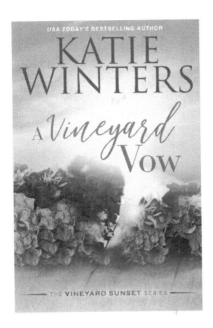

Other Books by Katie

Connect with Katie Winters

BookBub
Facebook
Newsletter

To receive exclusive updates from Katie Winters please sign up
to be on her Newsletter!
CLICK HERE TO SUBSCRIBE

Made in the USA
Middletown, DE
22 February 2023

25400343R00104